S0-BSM-038

"ARE YOU PAYING BACK GOOD DEEDS, OR JUST HUNGRY FOR A GOOD MAN?"

"No, this is for me," she replied, "because I've done nothing but think about you and hope you might come back this way. You're here, not the way I'd thought about your coming back but you're here."

He reached out, put a hand around the back of her neck, drew her to him. "And you're hungry," he said.

Her eyes flashed protest. "Not because there was nobody wanting. I just don't settle for less than I want."

"How do you decide what you want?"

"Something goes off deep inside, and I know. It's not hard if you know how to listen to yourself."

Just listen to yourself, he repeated silently. Right now he couldn't help but listen to the surge of desire within him . . .

SIGNET Brand Westerns You'll Enjoy

THE
HANGING TRAIL

by

Jon Sharpe

A SIGNET BOOK

NEW AMERICAN LIBRARY

TIMES MIRROR

PUBLISHER'S NOTE

This novel is a work of fiction. Names, characters, places, and incidents are either the product of the author's imagination or are used fictitiously, and any resemblance to actual persons, living or dead, events, or locales is entirely coincidental.

Copyright © 1980 by Jon Sharpe

A portion of chapter one of *The Hanging Trail* appeared in *Seven Wagons West*, the first of *The Trailsman* series.

SIGNET TRADEMARK REG. U.S. PAT. OFF. AND FOREIGN COUNTRIES REGISTERED TRADEMARK—MARCA REGISTRADA
HECHO EN CHICAGO, U.S.A.

SIGNET, SIGNET CLASSICS, MENTOR, PLUME, MERIDIAN AND NAL BOOKS are published by The New American Library, Inc., 1633 Broadway, New York, New York 10019

First Printing, July, 1980

1 2 3 4 5 6 7 8 9

PRINTED IN THE UNITED STATES OF AMERICA

The Trailsman

Beginnings . . . they bend the tree and they
mark the man. Skye Fargo was born when he
was eighteen. Terror was his midwife,
vengeance his first cry. Killing spawned Skye
Fargo, ruthless, cold-blooded murder. Out
of the acrid smoke of gunpowder still
hanging in the air, he rose, cried out a
promise never forgotten.

The Trailsman, they began to call him all
across the West: searcher, scout, hunter, the
man who could see where others only looked,
his skills for hire but not his soul, the man
who lived each day to the fullest, yet trailed
each tomorrow. Skye Fargo, the Trailsman,
the seeker who could take the wildness of a
land and the wanting of a woman and make
them his own.

*1861—the Free Territory of Wyoming,
just below the Oregon Trail*

1

The Ovaro pinto and the tall black-haired man on it might have been carved in stone. Only the man's eyes, lake-blue that had grown cold as blue quartz, moved, narrowed. The fight, such as it was, four burly men against a young girl and a boy no more than fifteen, had been going on when he came into sight of it over the ridge. The boy was lying on the ground now, beaten senseless, one of the men kneeling beside him with gun in hand. The other three had the girl, two holding her arms over her head on the ground, the third man standing over her, starting to lift her skirt.

They'd been too busy to notice the tall man nose the pinto down through the narrow passages between the rocks, his lips set in a thin line. Skye Fargo had been on his way to Pointed Rock, still ten miles away after a week's hard riding and the last of the day coming fast. He was late, the trip full of delays. He didn't need another one. Besides, he didn't normally interfere in private fights. Too often you found yourself helping the wrong side. But this one looked rotten, smelled rotten, felt rotten; he moved down closer, still staying behind the tall red-clay rock formations.

Howard Kent and Pointed Rock would have to wait. He'd been growing increasingly sorry he had decided to take up Howard Kent's call for help in

1

the letter, though the money the man had offered was still very attractive. But it had been a last-minute decision on his part, already filled with little problems, delays, irritations. And now these four big bastards doing a job on the girl and the boy. "Damn," he swore as he reached the level ground, glimpsed the scene through a space between the rocks. The girl, smooth, long legs exposed, kicked out at the man standing over her, a bear-shouldered man with a face full of little red veins. He dodged a kick, cursed.

"Hold her still, dammit," he yelled at the other two.

"We got her arms, Luke. Hell, we can't hold her legs, too," one of the others protested as the girl kicked out again. Skye Fargo cast a quick glance at her, saw only smooth, lithe legs as she continued to kick.

"Twist her arms," the one called Luke yelled, and the other two did as they'd been told. Fargo heard the girl's gasp of pain.

"Bastards. Rotten, stinking bastards," he heard the girl shout through her gasp. His eyes glinted at the big, bear-shouldered man. They were all too intent on the girl to notice anything else and Fargo's mind clicked off options. The two holding her had their hands full. The burly one with the red-veined face was about to be even more occupied. Only the one beside the boy could move quickly, his gun already out. Fargo returned his glance to Luke and saw the girl kick out again, a flash of yellow bloomers visible.

"I'll kill you," she hissed.

Luke roared with glee. "Real little hellcat, ain't she?" he said, and moved closer to the girl, side-stepped another kick. But this time he bent over, smashed the back of his hand across her face. Her cry

2

of pain was instant, fighting through the fury, but she again kicked out at him. He took the blow on the side of his thigh, bent over, and picked up a riding crop. He stepped closer to the girl and avoided her kicks as she twisted her torso to reach him.

"You tried using this on me, honey. That wasn't nice," he said with mock concern, and then, moving quickly, he brought the riding crop down hard against the girl's legs. Her scream was full of sharp pain as she automatically twisted her legs away from the blow. Luke leaped forward at once, half-fell over her, hands reaching up and ripping the yellow bloomers down.

Cursing, the girl tried to get her knee up, but he was leaning down on her, pushing her thighs apart. He jammed the riding crop up between her thighs; she screamed, pulled her legs apart for an instant. It was enough for the man. He fell onto her, kept her legs apart now with his hands.

"Jesus, look at that beaver," he shouted gleefully. "Oh, this is gonna be good, real good."

The girl still tried to twist, but she was helpless, spread-eagled, the other two men holding her steady.

"I'm next, Luke," one of them yelled. "Don't use it all up."

"Hell, no, not this one. She's got plenty of life in her," Luke said, began to push himself forward as he unbuttoned his Levi's. "Look here, dolly. Look what Luke's got for you," he roared.

The girl screamed, fear pushing fury aside now.

"Let me put a bullet in the kid now," the fourth man said. "I want some of it, too."

"You'll get a chance to dip your stick," Luke called back. "You just stay there with him, Eddie. I ain't decided what we'll do with him yet."

The man called Luke started to move forward on the girl, keeping her legs open as he pushed upward,

3

his weight immobilizing her. As he edged to his goal, pumping upward, the girl screamed at the touch of him, and he tore her shirt open with one hand.

"Give it to her, Luke boy," one of the ones holding her arms called out.

Skye let a deep sigh escape from him as he swung from the pinto, landed on the balls of his feet. He unholstered the big Remington .44, moved to the edge of the rocks. His eyes swept the scene again, flicked to the man beside the boy, measured distances, clicked seconds in his mind for a moment longer. He heard the girl's scream rise suddenly, stepped forward alongside the edge of the rock.

"That's enough," he said, the quiet steel of his voice cutting through the girl's screams and the shouting of the men. The man atop the girl halted, stayed lying over her, and the other two looked up. They were as if frozen, a tableau of surprise. The one called Luke, not moving from atop the girl, turned his head to look back at the tall figure with the shock of black hair that fell loosely over his forehead. His veined face took on a frown.

"Who the hell are you?" he rasped out.

"Friend of the family," Fargo said quietly.

"Shit you are. You got two seconds to get your ass out of here, mister," the man growled, still staying atop the girl.

"You got one second to get your ass off her," Fargo said softly.

"Eddie," the man called out, exactly as Fargo had expected he would. Fargo whirled, firing as he did, before the fourth man could bring his gun up. The big Remington all but tore the man's head off, his body arching backward with the force of the bullet's impact. But Fargo was whirling back again, firing, but not at the bear-shouldered man. Luke was still busy half-driving, half-rolling from atop the girl.

4

Fargo fired over him at the other two, who had dropped the girl's arms and had their guns half-out. His shot caught the nearest one full in the chest, and he heard the man's guttural gasp as his breastbone splintered. The other one dove backward, squid-like, twisting, trying to save himself, survival the only thing on his mind now.

It was time to dive, and Fargo vaulted sideways, behind the safety of the rock as the shot sent stone splinters flying a half-inch from his head. The one called Luke had gotten his gun out, came up firing; but Fargo's split-second timing had allowed for every precious instant, and now, behind the red-clay rock, he ran to the other end, dropped to one knee, sent a shot flying as he looked out. The girl lay face buried in the dirt, arms covering her head, and the bear-shouldered man was scrambling backward up a small slope, lunged sideways as Fargo's shot slammed into the ground. The fourth one was out of sight. Fargo saw the one called Luke reach a rock cover, dart behind it. He sent another shot after the disappearing figure, saw it slam into the man's ankle. A half-curse, half-cry of pain echoed at once and the burly figure slid backward, clutching at his ankle, then bringing his gun up, firing wildly. Fargo, on one knee, moved a half-inch to the right, squinted along the sighting groove of the big Remington. The man was diving behind the rock cover again as Fargo fired. The shot hit his right elbow and Fargo saw the bone shatter.

"Oh, Jesus," the man screamed, fell backward, slid down the slope as his gun fell from a hand without nerves or muscles. The man rolled from the slope, following the gun as it clattered down. He landed almost at the girl's head, and Fargo saw her look up, spring forward at once, her hand closing around the gun. Wholly up on one elbow, she faced the man.

5

Fargo dived forward, but she was firing, at almost point-blank range, emptying the gun into the burly figure. Fargo saw the man's body shudder as each of the bullets slammed into it. The girl was still firing, still pulling a trigger that clicked hollowly on empty cylinders as Fargo reached her.

"No good, stinking son of a bitch." She was sobbing as she continued to pull the trigger, the gun still aimed at the lifeless figure. Fargo closed his hand over hers, slowly pried the gun from her fingers.

"Easy, now, easy," he said as his eyes searched the top of the rocks. The fourth one was still up there someplace, and then he heard the sound of the horse whinny, followed by pounding hooves. The fourth was hightailing it as fast as his horse could carry him. Fargo holstered the Remington, looked down to find the girl gone. He found her beside the boy, cradling his head in his arms. With the tail of her shirt, she wiped blood from his face.

"Jerry, can you hear me? Jerry, please say something," she was murmuring. Fargo reached her in one long stride, knelt down, and lifted the boy's eyelids, felt the young cheeks. The skin was cold, clammy cold, and the girl watched him with tearstains on her cheeks.

"He could go into shock damn quick," Fargo said. "He needs a warm blanket and his feet up high, his wounds treated, and he needs it fast."

"Help me get him home?" the girl asked.

"Where are your horses?" Fargo said.

"Over there," she answered, gesturing behind a line of rocks.

"Get them. I'll ride him with me," Fargo said. As she ran to fetch the horses, he lifted the boy, carried him to where the pinto waited. He lifted the boy onto the saddle, held him there with one hand as he

6

swung up behind him, letting the slender figure slump back against his chest. The girl appeared with two stumpy horses and Fargo saw her halt at the figure of Luke. She reached down, made a face as she avoided the blood on the man's body, pulled a cloth money bag from his pocket, and tucked it into her waist.

"It's ours," she said, chin tilted upward. "He took it from me." She swung onto the horse, started through a space between the rocks. "This way. It's not far."

"It best not be," Fargo said, nodded a head toward the limp form against him. "How old is he?"

"Fourteen," the girl said. "He's my kid brother. I'm Arlene Hargrove."

"Skye Fargo," he answered, looked at the girl more carefully as she swung her horse beside the pinto. She had a strong face, high cheekbones and a wide mouth, even with her face pale white and tensed. Not pretty, he reflected, but a face with clean, strong lines. Handsome was a better word. In a dozen years the strong cheekbones might make it rawboned, but now it was young and handsome. Her shirt, dark red plaid, hung loosely over modest breasts, and he'd already glimpsed the beauty of the rest of her. "Who were those buzzards?" he asked, saw her jaw grow tight.

"Some of the raiders," she said. "That's all I know."

"Who are the raiders?"

"Nobody knows, really, except that they've come to call them that," Arlene Hargrove told him.

"Why?" Skye asked.

"They come, hit, raid, and disappear," she said.

"For no reason?"

"Oh, they've got reasons," she said.

"Why were they doing a job on you?" he asked.

"We were coming back from Pointed Rock with the money from Mr. Kent," Arlene told him, led the way down into a small valley.

"Money? From Howard Kent?" Fargo frowned.

"For the herd my uncle sold him last week," she said. "I live with my uncle, Terence Morphy. He's one of the small ranchers who sell their stock to Mr. Kent. He pays us a good price and then drives the herds to Abilene when he gets a large enough lot. The small ranchers could never afford the money and the time it takes to drive a big herd down to Abilene."

Fargo kept the frown from his face, but he listened carefully to the girl's every word. Perhaps she was handing him the reason he'd been summoned to Pointed Rock. "And these raiders, they don't want the small ranchers to deal with Howard Kent," he said.

"That's right," Arlene Hargrove said. "Uncle Terence is one of the few who still sell to Mr. Kent. The raiders have killed or scared away most of the others."

Skye Fargo's face held a moment of quiet thought. The letter from Howard Kent was definitely taking on shape and form. The money he'd offered was making sense now, too. Howard Kent was apparently growing desperate for help. The flat-roofed ranch house came into view, chasing away further speculation. Fargo's eyes scanned the building, badly in need of a coat of paint, the weathered barn attached to it, two smaller outbuildings nearby, and a large corral bordered by stake-and-rider fences. A man emerged as they rode up, a round face with little hair over it, flooding with concern as he saw the boy. Fargo swung from the saddle, helped carry the boy into the house and onto a trundle bed.

"What happened?" the man said.

8

"The raiders," Arlene answered. "We'd be dead, I guess, except for this man. His name's Fargo, Skye Fargo."

"I'll thank you later, mister," the man said. "Fetch a blanket, Arlene," but the girl was already bringing it.

"Keep his feet up," Fargo said. He stepped back, let the girl and the man work on the boy, clean the blood from his bruises, keep him warm. The man took down a jar with a salve in it, began to apply it to the cuts and bruises all over the boy's head, chest, and arms.

"Nothing broken, far as I can tell," Fargo said.

"Then this salve will help the hurt places. Balm of Gilead buds, boiled-down pine pitch, and Jamaica rum," Terence said. "Ain't no better salve anywhere."

The boy remained the same for a long while, but finally the signs of normal color began to return to his face. Fargo left the girl and her uncle and went outside, where the night had dropped over the land, the far hills a dark silhouette now against a star-swept sky. He leaned against the roughness of the wood outside the house, let thoughts float in his mind. He hadn't been going to come at all. Howard Kent wasn't one of his favorite people. Few even knew that he'd known the man before. Yet the money offered had been too good just to turn down out of hand. But curiosity as much as anything else had decided him to come, and now some of that curiosity had been satisfied. Kent would have more details to tell him, of course.

And there was one more reason he'd decided to come. Lily was in Pointed Rock and he couldn't remember how many years back he'd promised to come see her. He'd combine the two now. Seeing Lily again would make the trip worthwhile, even if he turned down Howard Kent's proposition. A simpler, more enjoyable job would be easy enough to pick up here. They'd be bidding for his services if he offered them, all those who knew the name of the Trailsman . . . and plenty did. Skye Fargo's eyes peered into the distance as though the hills weren't in the way.

The Oregon Trail lay directly to the north, the way to a new life for some, a new land with new hope. For others, the Oregon Trail was only a route to death. The early fur traders had first taken it, but only after Whitman and Parker trekked their way along it did the steady flow of settlers begin to follow. Many started back in Kansas, some even back in Independence, Missouri. More picked up the trail in Nebraska, where it moved alongside the Platte River. But all had to come into the Wyoming Territory, the high mountain country of Independence Rock, the Sweetwater River, and South Pass, the fierce, hard country that demanded more than most could give, fierce cold, burning heat, and the Arapaho and the Cheyenne.

Yet they came, the land-hungry and heart-poor, flocking to the Oregon Trail to search for a new life in a better place. Some made it all the way. Most turned back or settled for a place along the way, and many of those never lived long enough to regret their decisions. But still they came to the Oregon Trail, moving onward, wagon trains, families, and loners. That was the one thing the Indian never understood, the white man's driving need to expand, to find other lands, other places. He could understand the power of the white man's guns, the white man's warriors, the pony soldiers. He could understand those who came to hunt and to trap, even those who came to build and stay in one place during the terrible winters. But the white man's constant seeking, the driving need that kept more and more of them

10

coming, searching, going on despite death and famine and hardships of every kind—that the Indian could not comprehend.

Fargo grunted under his breath. He didn't understand it too well, either, but maybe that was the one-quarter Cherokee in him. Yet they kept coming, plodding the trail, and the red man's inability to understand that driving force would do more to destroy him than all the guns and soldiers one day.

He saw the shadowed figure of the girl materialize at the door, come toward him. "He's going to be all right," she said. "He'll be hurting a good while, but he'll get over it. Thanks to you, he's not dead. Nor me. They'd have killed me . . . afterward."

"Probably," Skye allowed.

"I owe you a lot," the girl said, her high cheekbones standing out over the dark shadows in her face, touched by the moonlight. "Stay the night with us," she said, and then, "with me."

"Gratitude?"

She shrugged, watched the big man's face soften in a smile, a rugged, handsome face of intensity and power.

"I have to get on," he said.

"There's more," she remarked.

It was his turn to shrug. "I'm not much on gratitude standing in for what ought to be," he told her.

The moonlight touched the side of her face as she studied him. "No, you wouldn't want that. I understand. What if I said it was more than gratitude?"

"I might believe it, some other time," he said.

Terence Morphy stepped out of the house, walked toward the girl and him. "I'm mighty beholden to you, Fargo," he said. "Arlene told me all of it. Anything I can do for you, just call."

"Obliged. You know anything more about these raiders and Howard Kent's troubles?" Fargo asked.

"No more'n Arlene told you. Anybody but Howard Kent would've been out of business by now," the man said.

"Meaning what?" Fargo questioned.

"Folks here owe Howard Kent, in town and out," the man said.

"Owe him what?"

"Loyalty, a fair shake, personal favors. He's been good to the small ranchers, carried plenty along when their cattle turned out poor, let them ride over hard times. I'm included," Terence Morphy said. "We've held on, a good many of us."

"And the others?" Fargo asked.

"Some paid the price for it. And some just took off, those with families to think about. Loyalty has its limits, I guess. Better to leave your land alive than stay on it dead," the man said.

"It seems that somebody's trying to run Howard Kent into the ground, and the way to do it is to chase off all his suppliers. That seems pretty damn clear," Fargo said. "You've a sheriff in Pointed Rock. Conley, Bloodhound Conley, they call him."

Terence Morphy shot a sideways smile. "Know Bloodhound, do you?"

"Not personally, but he's got a reputation. I hear he's proud of never having lost a prisoner."

"That's Bloodhound Conley," the man agreed with a half-chuckle.

"Can't he draw a bead on this thing?" Fargo asked. "On these raiders who just hit and disappear? Somebody's got to be behind it. It oughtn't to be that hard to know who'd gain most by breaking up Howard Kent's setup." Fargo frowned.

"Sure, there are a few who'd like to take over for Kent, see him cleared out and step in with their own people. Gil Dobles, for one. He's been trying for years to edge into the cattle drives Howard runs, but

12

nobody wants to sell to him. Aaron Elliman down at Hell's Beacon is another. Trouble is, the sheriff's had both of these spreads watched and he can't come up with a damn thing to tie either of them to this."

"But they're both close enough?" Fargo asked.

"Too close. It ought to be easy to trail these raiders in or out of either place if they are involved," Terence Morphy answered, frowned off into space. "I don't know how much longer I'll hang on. This, today, is hitting as close as I want to see, too damn close." He let a deep sigh lift his chest, looked at the big man in front of him. "So long as I'm here, you're welcome anytime, Fargo," he said, pushed his hand out.

"Thanks," Fargo said as he shook the worn hand. "Take care of the boy. He had a hard one today."

The girl moved, stepped closer as her uncle turned back to the house, and Fargo met her steady eyes, lingered for a moment at the angular handsomeness of her. "Will you come back this way?" she asked.

"Maybe. I'll stop by if I do," he said.

"I'd like that," Arlene Hargrove told him, simple honesty in her voice. She reached up on her toes, her mouth finding his, the kiss quick as a wink, soft as a summer wind. "For Jerry. For us all," she said.

Fargo turned and walked the few paces to the pinto, climbed into the saddle, turned once to wave at her. The light from the window caught at her with a soft-yellow glow, outlined the high comeliness of her face, the smooth line of her breasts. Maybe he would stop back, he thought. Maybe he just might do that. He turned the horse west toward Pointed Rock, disappeared in the darkness.

Directions with the letter had set Howard Kent's place just north of Pointed Rock, but it had grown too late to go there now. Besides, he wanted a little more thinking time on what he had learned from the girl and her uncle. He rode slowly, reached Pointed Rock, walked the pinto down the main street, dark and mostly deserted. But at the far end of the town, a square oasis of light beckoned, and he moved toward it as if he'd been there before. Lily's letters had described the town, the street, and her new place in detail. But that was when she'd first opened, before she had stopped writing.

He grunted, a wry sound. It had been long ago, or only yesterday, depending on how you reckoned the passage of time. The square of light grew larger, reached out into the street, became a frame building with a sign over the double swinging doors, LILY'S PALACE—DRINKS, FOOD & ENTERTAINMENT. Fargo smiled in the darkness. He wondered if Lily would be angered when she learned he hadn't come just to see her. He walked the pinto on a few yards to the stable, dismounted, looked inside. It was a clean stable, well-kept, probably owned by Lily, he pondered.

The stableboy came out, rubbing sleep from his eyes, a thin-legged youth nursing the beginnings of a beard. His eyes came alive as he looked at the Ovaro pinto, black from head to withers and croup to hind legs, solid white in between, a striking horse with the stance of a Thoroughbred. The hand-tooled Mexican leather saddle with the decorated rosaderos and cantle held his glance, also.

"Got room?" Fargo asked, snapping the boy's attention back to him.

"Yes, yes, sir, always for the likes of him," the boy said. "How long?"

"Don't know, a few days at least," Fargo said. He slapped a hand on the saddle. "Saddle-soap it before morning?" he asked.

"Yes, sir, do it myself. Give me something to do during the night. Be pleasure to saddle-soap this one," the boy answered.

"Good," the big black-haired man said, strode away on long, loping steps, reached the building with the sound of the tinny piano coming from inside. He pushed the double doors open, and the bright light and the sound rushed over him as though it were an ocean wave. The sounds blended together, became one, the harsh, low sound of the men's voices, the piano, and the shriller sound of the women's laughter cutting through all else. Fargo's eyes moved slowly across the large main room, big chandeliers allowing plenty of bright light, a polished wood bar taking up one wall, the tables scattered across the floor. In the room beyond, the gaming tables covered in bright green that vibrated under the light. Two dark-oak stairways at each end of the main room led upstairs to the private rooms there. If he knew Lily, her place would be run with class, her girls a notch above the average.

His eyes passed over the men and the girls at the main-room tables, most drinking, some wrapped together. He halted as his eyes spied her, near the end of the bar, talking to a man in a frock coat. He

15

moved through the crowd toward her, a smile in his eyes. She looked the same, blond hair piled high atop her head, a round-cheeked face, and a full figure. Lily Madigan was one of the only women he'd ever known who could be brassy and not cheap. She wore a black-velvet gown, her rounded shoulders bare, a line of velvet buttons holding in her large breasts yet allowing enough flesh to escape. She was still talking to the man as he came up behind her.

"Five years hasn't hurt you at all," he remarked quietly, saw her stiffen, her mouth fall open. She turned slowly, her brown eyes starting to widen. Her full red lips tried to form his name, failed, finally found voice.

"I'm seeing things. Hearing and seeing," she half-whispered.

He laughed. "No," he said, and suddenly her arms were tight around him, her fullness pressing into his chest. As her lips found his mouth, a saddlebag full of memories fell open.

"Skye Fargo, damn you," she whispered. "You finally made it." She clung for another moment, and his hand rubbed along her back. She was still a damn lot of woman, he thought. Lily Madigan had never been the ordinary dance-hall girl. More brains, more drive, more everything. She pulled back, her eyes moving over him, eyes that were both shrewd and warm at once. "Better-looking than ever," she commented. "I've kept hearing about the Trailsman."

"Have you?" He laughed as his arms stayed holding her waist.

"Men come from all over to a place like this, each with a story to tell, and after a few drinks they tell it. Skye Fargo's name came up often enough. You've been into a lot of hard places," she said, and her eyes narrowed a fraction, took on concern. "Still searching, aren't you?" she asked.

He nodded slowly. "I'll find them, one day. I keep hearing things, too," he said. "Promises that still need keeping."

Lily Madigan took his arm, led the way to a side table. "Let's sit here for a spell. We'll go upstairs later. I always like to keep an eye on things for a few hours," she said. "By God, I still can't believe you're here." She seemed to be sucking her round cheeks into a mock severity. "I shouldn't be talking to you at all—all these years and not even a message. I wouldn't be if I wasn't so damn glad to see you." The woman sat back in the chair, put her elbows on the round hardwood table, gestured to the air with one hand. "What do you think of the place, Skye?"

"Very nice, Lily. Very impressive. But I expected as much. You always had a flair. And a touch of class," he added.

Her hand pressed his arm and her brown eyes grew dreamy. "It's like old times sitting here with you, Skye," she remembered softly. "Do you ever see any of the old bunch from Elbow Creek?"

"Ollie Hawkins is dead," the big man said. "An Indian arrow found him."

"Ollie had been on borrowed time for years," the woman said. She brought up other names, places out of another time, and they plunged backward into old stories and old remembrances. The noise of the big room became a background hum as they closed out the rest of the world. One of the girls—young, slender, an open, pretty face—stopped by to ask Lily a question, and as she left, Skye saw the man moving toward them, making his way around the crowded tables. He was a tall man, as tall as himself, Fargo guessed, with maybe ten to twelve years more on him. He had a straight nose, a lined, serious face with eyes gray as a junco's wing. A leather vest sported a silver star.

17

" 'Evening, Lily," he said as he halted at the table.

"Sit down, Clyde," the woman said, nodded to Fargo. "Old friends have come calling. This is Skye Fargo. Skye . . . Sheriff Conley."

The gray-eyed man eased himself in a chair, nodded at Fargo. "The Trailsman," he commented. "Heard about you, Fargo."

Fargo smiled. "Heard good or heard bad?"

Sheriff Conley half-smiled, and even his smile was serious, Fargo thought. "Some of both. You don't mind making your own laws," the sheriff said.

"When there's need to," Fargo answered evenly.

"There's no need here," Conley said pleasantly. "I try to keep an orderly town. A lot of folks stop here before setting onto the Oregon Trail. I like to leave the taste of law and order with them. They'll be without it for five months or more."

"Something to hold on to for them," Fargo said.

"That's right," Sheriff Conley agreed. "Visiting Lily bring you here?"

Skye glanced at Lily, saw her eyes waiting. "Partly. Howard Kent asked me to come see him," he said.

"I might've known it wasn't just me," the woman said.

"Howard sent for you?" The sheriff's lips pursed for a moment. "Can't say I blame him. Did he tell you why?"

"No, but I've heard some talk," Fargo answered.

"Did you hear he got married last month?" Lily asked, and Skye's eyebrows lifted. "Yep, married a gal maybe thirty years younger, but he's happy and that's what counts. Real good-looker, she is."

"Howard deserves his happiness," Sheriff Conley put in. "He's been good to this town, spent part of his profits from the cattle drives on things for the town. Folks here are mighty fond of Howard Kent."

"Not everybody," Fargo remarked, and saw Con-

18

ley's mouth tighten for a moment, the gray eyes harden to slate.

"I expect we'll be talking some more, after you've seen Howard," the sheriff said.

"I expect we might," Fargo agreed.

Conley rose, nodded to him and the woman, walked back across the crowded room, a slow, powerful walk that carried quiet tenacity in it. "So that's Bloodhound Conley," Fargo murmured. "I'd guess the name fits."

"It does. He's a good man, though—hard, but fair. But no man to cross," Lily said.

Fargo watched the tall man leave the building and his eyes narrowed in thought. "I wonder if he knows that Kent and me had hard words when he was a district judge," Fargo mused aloud.

"When those gunslingers wiped out your family?" Lily asked.

Fargo nodded. "Howard Kent was district judge then. He had the power to authorize a federal posse, but he didn't do it. We had hard words then, almost came to more than words."

"Yes, I remember. But it turned out, later, that he didn't have the manpower," Lily said.

"That's right, but he came close to getting himself shot over it," Fargo said.

"I'd say Conley knows about that. He's got a file-cabinet kind of mind," Lily said. She frowned at Fargo. "Just why did you come here? You still don't think much of Howard Kent."

"Curiosity, I guess," Fargo said. "And I did him a wrong, almost put daylight through him because of it. Maybe I figured I owed him a visit, anyway. And you, too."

"Well, we're going to see that one of those visits is worthwhile," the woman said. "You're not too tired from the day's ride, I hope."

"Not after seeing you." He laughed.

Lily Madigan rose, beckoned to a young girl in a red-silk gown. "You're in charge, Rosie," she told the girl. "This is Skye Fargo. We'll be upstairs, in my rooms, if you need me." She turned to Fargo. "Give me a minute to talk to my bartender," she said, hurried off.

The younger woman cast a long glance at the big man, and he felt her eyes on him, looked at her. "You must be something special," she said, undisguised awe in her voice. "Lily doesn't go to her rooms with anyone."

Memories touched his slow smile. "We go back some," he said. "To Elbow Creek. A no-good heel tried to ruin her place there. I helped her get rid of him. Lily's not the kind to forget."

"You've got to be special in more ways than that," Rosie commented doggedly.

"I try," Fargo answered as Lily returned, linked her arm in his, and steered him up one of the two dark-oak stairways to the upper floor. Her room was large, dark-red velvet on the walls and full of flounces, on the chairs, the sofa, the curtains. The window, he noted, looked out over Main Street, now only a dark ribbon. She came and halted before him, looking pretty much the way she did five years ago.

"The way we used to, Fargo," she said, and he smiled. Going back more than the last five years, Lily had been the one to teach him more than he knew, then. She waited, standing still, and he reached out, slowly began to undo the buttons down the front of her bodice. The velvet gown came apart at once, the rise of her breasts expanding, then her large, creamy mounds cascading free of the gown. He reached down, lifted the dress up over her head, tossed it onto a chair. His hands undid the bows of the undergarment, slowly, deliberately, let the gar-

20

ment fall away. Then he unsnapped the black-net stockings from the garter belt, pushed them down until she kicked them free.

She stood before him, nude, her full breasts rising slowly with the rhythm of her breathing. Her hips, wide and womanly, stomach slightly curved out, the small sign of passing years. He slipped down to his knees, took first one full breast and then the other in his mouth, sucked gently, let his tongue caress the tiny little circles of dark pink. The nipples rose at once, grew firm, thrusting out for more. "Oh, God, Skye, the way it was, make it the way it was." Lily Madigan gasped, and Fargo heard the hint of desperation in her plea. He took in more of the soft-cream mounds, pulled harder, and she gasped again; then he moved down, painting an invisible line with his lips along the rise of her belly, down lower, sinking his face into the still-small dark triangle.

Lily Madigan let herself go backward, onto the wide bed, lifting her pelvis for him, her hands clasping around his neck, pulling her to him. "Yes, yes, yes," he heard her harsh whisper. "Oh, Skye, Skye, remember, remember." He answered, remembered with his lips, his tongue, and the woman rose up, cried out hoarsely, twisted and quivered for him, and as her hands pulled against his back, he moved atop her, resting himself against her softness as she moved under him, trying to find him, her hips rising, twisting, the hunted seeking the hunter. He kept back from the sweet trap, remembering, and Lily Madigan grew frantic, pumping her body upward wildly. Suddenly, the long, low cry began to spiral from her and he moved quickly, thrust into her. The cry became a call of pleasure. "Oh, yes, Fargo, Fargo, that's how it always was," she murmured into his shoulder as he stayed with her. But it was only a beginning, the beginnings they always

21

had, and now he stayed in her, moving slowly, tantalizingly, the way she wanted him to move, the way she had taught him in another place and another time.

She gathered herself again, more slowly this time, always slower the second time, but no less total as she dug fingers into his broad, muscled back, pressed herself hard against his thrusting. Finally she lay back, held his face against her breasts, time turned back once again. He slept in her arms until the small hours of the morning, when he woke to her hands massaging him, stroking, caressing, arousing, and he rolled onto her once again and the dark became filled with only the soft-harsh sounds of her cries. Later, beside him, her hand cradling, she breathed into his ear.

"I'm glad I held back for so long," she said, then added honestly, "Most of the time, anyway."

"You were never one for taking on anybody," he reminded her, and she nodded into his chest, curled her full-bodied figure tight against him, and slept. It had been more than good, all of it, and Fargo let the satisfied exhaustion take hold: he slept hard, in a soft bed, for the first time in weeks.

When he woke again, he sat bolt upright, sun flooding the room. He rose at once, one long stride taking him to the mirrored dresser and the note propped up between perfume bottles and powder boxes, hairpins and curlers. He read it aloud: "Breakfast and me waiting downstairs. Lily." He found warm water in a big metal washtub and enjoyed the luxury of it, dressed, and went down the dark-oak stairway to the big room below. The room was empty, tables neat, floor swept, and then he saw the small table in a corner, Lily sitting there going over a sheaf of bills. He walked to her and her lips opened for his kiss.

"It's good to make love to a man you really like," she said.

"Or a woman you can call a friend, too," Fargo countered as he sat down. A young black brought wheatcakes and butter, maple syrup and coffee, vanished on soundless feet.

"Marcy," Lily said. "Found her way here from Georgia. Good girl. She'll make a place for herself somewhere."

"I hear there's talk of secession in the South," Fargo said. "But talk's cheap down there."

"You going to see Howard Kent now?" Lily asked. "Say hello for me."

"His new bride, she from around here?" Fargo asked.

"No, never saw her till she came here looking for land. Seems her daddy left her some money. She found Howard Kent and got more than land." Lily laughed. "Some girls are just lucky. Made a real play for him, she did, and won."

Fargo finished breakfast, stood up, saw the instant anxiousness in Lily Madigan's eyes. "You'll be back no matter what you decide about Kent," she asked.

"I'll be back," he told her, "one way or the other."

3

Fargo expected Howard Kent's ranch to be big, the corrals spacious, the house sumptuous. It was all of that, the house low, stone. The architect had a little

Mexican in him, Fargo suspected, taking in the tall, arched windows, the wrought-iron grillwork, and the wide, spacious flagstone terraces that surrounded the house. But no one had prepared him for the new Mrs. Kent. Perhaps they couldn't have if they'd tried.

She was standing on one of the wide flagstone terraces, alongside a stucco post, framed by the open doorway to the house behind her. There was little wonder she'd snared Howard Kent. She could damn well snare anybody, Fargo thought. He'd seen a lot of damn beautiful women but never any more breathtaking. Flame-red hair framed a face with brown eyes, a thin nose, and fine-lined lips, the lower one fuller than the upper. She had cream-alabaster skin that seemed to glow softly and she wore the flame hair long with a soft natural wave to it. A deep-green wool shirt rested on breasts that turned upward sharply at the tips, over a slender, long waist, and legs encased in riding britches. She was in her early twenties, he guessed. Only her eyes disturbed the perfection of her. They held his boldly, almost imperiously, but there was something behind them, a kind of restlessness, something he couldn't quickly pin down.

He glimpsed the two cowhands crossing the corral as he swung from the saddle. "Skye Fargo," he said to the young woman.

"I'm Crystal Kent," she said, a touch of coolness in her tone.

"I figured as much," the Trailsman remarked.

Her eyebrows lifted a fraction. "Did you? Why?" she asked.

"I was told you were more than just good-looking," he said.

The brown eyes softened for a moment. She nodded in acceptance, let her eyes take in the

24

breadth and height of the man before her, the black hair that fell casually over his forehead, the strong, lean, intense face, and the lake-blue eyes.

"Mr. Kent expects me," Skye said. Something returned to the brown eyes, the quality that lay behind the surface coolness of them.

"You were expected last night," she said.

"The trip took longer, one thing and another," Fargo said.

"Unfortunately, Howard had to go away this morning. Business. He'll be back tomorrow night. Come back then and he'll be here to see you," Crystal Kent answered.

Fargo pursed his lips. "Tomorrow night," he echoed.

"Not before nine. I know Howard will want to rest some after his trip before seeing anyone," she said.

"Understandable," Fargo said, almost followed with a remark about age catching up to a man, but held his tongue. He peered at the young woman. The restlessness was in her eyes as she looked away, returned her gaze to him again. More than restlessness, almost an uneasiness, he decided. She was most likely still uneasy in her new role and probably all too aware that people talked about the young-woman-and-older-man marriage.

"All right, tomorrow night," he said. "Not before nine. I'll be here."

"Thank you," she said, her faint smile cool. "I'll tell him that when he returns."

Fargo turned from her, swung into the saddle, and waved at her. She didn't return the wave, but he felt her eyes watching him until he rode out of sight where the road curved. He rode back to Pointed Rock, not so much disappointed as annoyed. Lily was both surprised and happy to see him.

25

"I hope he doesn't come back for a week," she said. "So you met the new Mrs. Kent. Impressed? Most men are."

"Yes, but I think she's unsure of herself yet," Fargo said.

"She's young, that's all. It takes a while to become sure of yourself. Some people never do," Lily said, and Fargo had to agree with the truth in her words. Lily's hand pressed his. "And I've another day with you. Let's not waste it."

He went with her, and no moment of the day was wasted, none of her senses or the appetites denied. It was night when he came downstairs again with Lily, the gaming tables in full swing, the main room crowded, the bar busy. She had things to check on and left him at her private table. The tall gray-eyed man came in, moved through the crowd, the visit a nightly routine, obviously. Conley halted at the table, the question in his eyes.

"Didn't get to see him," Fargo told the man, and gave him the reasons, saw Conley's frown appear.

"That's not like Howard. He'd know a man coming a good distance might be a day late. He'd allow for that," the sheriff commented.

"Well, he didn't," Fargo snapped.

"Not like him," the sheriff repeated, moved on, circled the main room, paused to talk with Lily, and finally left. Fargo felt the wave of impatience sweep over him, triggered by Conley's words. Kent should have allowed for his being late a day or so, and Fargo remembered how the man had always been a mite imperious. His annoyance at having made the trip pushed at him again. If Kent didn't return by tomorrow night, that'd be the end of it. He'd pick up and leave, enjoyable as Lily would make staying. He ordered a bottle brought to the table, and by the night's end he'd drunk enough to sleep hard, Lily's breasts a warm pillow.

The irritation stayed, was with him when he woke the next morning, and he busied himself helping Lily with chores, fixing a table that had broken a leg, taking the buckboard to get supplies, making the day pass as quickly as he could. He was outside watching the night lower itself over the town when she came up to him. "You've been itchy as a horse-hair blanket all day," she remarked.

"Sorry. I don't like waiting around," he answered.

"That's not all," Lily said. "I know you, remember, Skye Fargo. Something about this Kent thing isn't setting right."

He laughed. "You know me," he agreed.

"Have you thought that perhaps Howard Kent wants to see you about something else?" she asked.

"It crossed my mind. I'll know soon enough," he said.

Lily's hand took his. "Come inside. I'll buy you a drink on finding out," she said. "I'll drink to your staying around." He made no comment and knew she expected none. They had the drink in warm quietness.

It was a little after nine when the pinto walked around the curve in the road nearing the Kent ranch, the moon bathing horse and rider in silver gray. The only sound was the soft step of the horse's hooves as the low long silhouette of the ranch came into view, the windows tall arches of yellow light. He halted at the hitching post, dropped the reins over it, and stepped onto the stone terrace. He was just about to life the door knocker when the portal opened and Crystal Kent nodded to him from the doorway, flame-red hair shimmering against a dress of deep blue cut low enough to show the round curve of

27

cream-alabaster mounds. She was every bit as striking as when he'd first seen her.

"Come in," she said as Fargo pulled his upraised hand back to his side. "Howard is in the study. Please follow me." The brown eyes touched his for an instant and turned quickly away. It was still there, he told himself as he followed her into the house, something still behind the dark orbs. He let himself enjoy the way she moved, an unbroken, smooth glide, no jiggling, bouncing rear. She halted at the open doorway of a large room, gestured for him to enter as she stepped back. Again, her eyes held his for the briefest of moments, flicked away uncomfortably. The quick darting glance did not go with the cool imperiousness of her beauty, but he dismissed further thoughts about her and strode into the room. Howard Kent, behind a heavy oak desk, rose to his feet in front of a paneled wall of books and mounted antelope head trophies. The man's large leonine head was the same, showing little signs of the years, his hair silver as it had always been.

"Well, Fargo, come in, come in," Howard Kent said in the deep resonant voice Fargo remembered so well. "Sorry I wasn't here when you came last night."

Fargo shrugged, let his eyes take in the large carpeted room, each side flanked by three tall, arched windows opening out to the night breeze. "You look well," he commented.

"You, too," Howard Kent returned, both men aware of a stiffness in the moment, both with smiles a little too forced.

"You've done well since retiring from the bench," Fargo commented. "Till lately."

Howard Kent's heavy face broke into a wry smile. "You've heard about that, have you?"

"Just talk," Fargo answered.

"I've heard that you're still searching," the man remarked.

"That's right," Fargo answered.

"You don't intend raking up old differences between us, I hope," Howard Kent said.

"No," Fargo said evenly.

"Good. I was wondering about that when Crystal told me you'd stopped in," the man said.

Fargo felt the frown touch his face at once. "What's that mean?" he asked.

"Nothing more than that, a thought that came to me," Howard Kent said. "Are you just passing through this way?"

The frown grew into a sudden uneasiness. "Passing through?" he echoed.

"Yes, passing through," the man repeated, waited.

Fargo felt the chill course through him. Something was very wrong. "I'm here because of the letter," he said.

Kent frowned. "What letter?" he asked.

The chill was growing into a prickling along the back of his neck. "The letter you sent me, asking me to come here," he said evenly.

"I never sent you a letter. I never asked you to come here," Howard Kent said, brows lowering.

The big black-haired man's eyes sent blue shafts out. "You playing games with me?" he growled.

"No," the other man snapped, bristling.

"You change your mind?" Fargo demanded. "Then just out and say it."

"I didn't change my mind about anything. I don't have any idea what you're talking about, Fargo," Howard Kent protested. Fargo caught the flash of flame-red hair as the girl entered the room. She halted just inside the door, her face full of apprehension.

"Is everything all right, Howard?" she asked.

"Yes, my dear, quite all right," Kent said. They were his last words. The men appeared in the open arched windows, six of them, one in each window on both sides of the room. They fired from where they stood in the windows, the room exploding in a hail of bullets. Fargo dived for cover, aiming to land back of a big heavy chair. He hit the ground, rolled, came up behind the chair, staying low. He saw that all the bullets had been aimed at one place, saw Howard Kent's body buckle, twist, fall across the desk, and then slowly slide to the floor, one hand clawing, taking the papers and desk blotter with him. He sank to the floor, fell on his back.

"Goddamn," Fargo said, whirled to get off a shot at the nearest window. But the window was empty and his glance flashed to the other arches. They were empty also and the sound of horses galloping away came from just outside. He straightened up, leaped onto the nearest open windowsill, the .44 raised. But only the dark hulk of fleeting horsemen, too far out of sight and range, met his eyes. He spun, leaped down from the window. Crystal Kent stood flattened against the wall near the door, her eyes wide with horror, her hands clasped to her face. Fargo ran past her to where Kent lay in a circle of blood that ran out of five holes in him. He knelt down, tried to find a pulse, a hint of breath, pulled his lips back as he found neither. Howard Kent was very dead, the leonine head still cast in surprise and pain.

Fargo stood up, drew a deep breath. The attack had taken perhaps ten, fifteen seconds, a savage, efficient operation, planned to the split second. They'd appeared and vanished almost in one motion. His eyes spied the gun lying on the floor near the window. He went to it, picked it up, saw it was empty, a heavy Dragoon Colt, still hot. One of the gunslingers had dropped it. His eyes went to Crystal Kent again.

She was still against the wall, hands still clasped to her face, and he started to walk toward her when he heard the sounds of horses racing to a halt outside. The Remington was in his hand again in a split second as he listened to voices, the sounds of men dismounting, and then the sheriff's orders, Conley's voice unmistakable through the others.

Fargo holstered the Remington, turned to the door as Conley rushed in, four men behind him, two wearing deputy's badges. Conley shot him a glance as he rushed to Kent, bent down over the blood-soaked form. When he rose, the gray eyes were slate, his face tight. "What happened?" he rasped.

"We were talking," Fargo began.

The girl's scream cut off the rest of his answer. "He did it," she cried out. "He killed Howard."

Fargo felt his jaw drop open as he turned to stare at Crystal Kent, astonishment freezing his voice. Crystal Kent's alabaster face was pink, her eyes on Conley. Fargo heard the sheriff's quiet command: "Get his gun." He started to reach for the Remington, felt two of the deputies behind him, their guns poking into his back. One reached over, unholstered the Remington.

Fargo found his voice, stared at the young woman. Her brown eyes wide, round, flashed at him for an instant. "What the hell is this?" he spit at her.

She spun around to Conley. "I came in just as he started shooting. I couldn't stop him," she said.

"You're lying," Fargo shouted.

The girl ignored him, half-fell forward to Conley, clutched at him as he caught her. She gasped words at him between sobs. "He had two guns. He emptied one," she said. "There it is, on the floor. He was shouting at Howard, calling him names. That's when I came in."

Fargo stared at the scene. He didn't believe what

31

he was hearing. He looked at Conley, saw the quiet rage in the man's face. "She's lying, goddammit. I didn't kill him. We were talking when six gunslingers burst in and started blazing away."

Crystal Kent shot a glance at him, clasped her hand to her face. "My God. Oh, my God," she gasped out, and Fargo watched her knees buckle as she began to collapse. Conley caught her, swung her up in his arms, and carried her to a leather settee.

"Tie him up," he yelled at his men. "If he tries anything, kill him." Fargo felt hands pull his arms back, the rope being tied around his wrists behind him. He saw Crystal Kent revive, shake the flame-red hair, sit up on one elbow. Conley stayed with her. "Easy, there, it's all right," the sheriff murmured.

"Goddammit, she's lying, all of it's a stinking lie," Fargo shouted.

The girl pressed her face against Conley's shoulder, sobbed into it.

"Take him outside," the sheriff barked, and Fargo was pulled roughly into the wide hallway. "Bastard," one of the men snarled. In the hall, at the far end, a woman, heavyset with the flat, broad face of Indian-Mexican blood, stood beside an elderly man, wringing a large kerchief in her hands. Fargo saw three more men enter, stand with the woman, peer at him. Some of Kent's cowhands, he surmised. He could hear Cyrstal Kent still sobbing out words to Conley, too low to catch, but the little bitch was doing a good job. Fargo eyed the doorway, the nearest open window. Too far. Any attempt to escape would be suicide. Conley probably had one or two more men outside. His eyes went back to the woman and the cowhands at the far end of the corridor, saw the grim anger in their faces.

Conley came out of the room, beckoned to the older woman. "Conchita, come here and take care of

Mrs. Kent," he called. As the woman moved toward the study, he turned to Fargo, gray eyes boring into the Trailsman. "You're going to hang, mister. You can be sure of that," he hissed.

"I didn't shoot him, dammit. She's lying her damn head off," Fargo yelled at the man's cold face.

"Now, why would she lie about a thing like that?" Conley said.

"I don't know, but she's sure as hell doing it," Fargo flung back.

"You came here to settle old scores," Conley said. "Howard Kent never sent for you. That's why he wasn't here last night. I knew there was something wrong about that. I said it then. He'd have allowed for your being late if he'd sent for you."

"Listen, Kent said he hadn't sent for me, so I guess maybe he hadn't. But somebody wrote me using his name. I was set up for this," Fargo said. He saw the disbelief in Conley's face and heard himself how strange the story sounded; he wondered if he'd believe it if their roles were reversed.

"You twist pretty good, Fargo," the sheriff said. "But Mrs. Kent told me she heard you ask him for money and he refused. That's why you came here, to lean on him for money. When he refused, you decided to settle old grudges."

Fargo's eyes moved past Conley as Crystal Kent came out of the room, holding on to the older woman's arm. Her eyes flashed to his, turned away at once. "Goddamn you, you stinking little bitch. Come back here and tell the truth," Fargo shouted at her. He started forward, felt the blow that caught him across the back of the neck. Hands tied behind him, he stumbled forward, landed on his knees. Conley's hands grasped his shirtfront, yanked him up. The man's eyes blazed fury.

"I'd like to string you up now," he hissed. "Only

we don't do things that way here. Judge Brown will be back in a day or two. He'll sentence you all nice and proper, and then I'll put the rope around your goddamn neck myself."

He flung the big man from him and Fargo fell backward, into the hands of two of the deputies. They pulled at him, hauled him outside, and his ribs took a half-dozen hard thrusts from their gun barrels. He was lifted onto the pinto and a rope put around his neck. It stayed there, held by one of the men, as Conley mounted up, started to lead the procession back to town. Fargo discarded any thoughts of escape now. Conley would be happy to kill him at the first excuse. He had to wait for a better moment, watch for it to come, but now he thought only of a beautiful flame-haired young woman with eyes that had hidden not simply unrest but betrayal and deceit. Perhaps it was shame he had seen flickering behind the deep-brown orbs. That could mean something of itself. But what? And perhaps it hadn't been shame at all, only a fear of inadvertently tipping her hand.

Only one thing was clear. He had been set up. Very cleverly, he'd been made a part of something bigger and he had to figure out how the pieces all fit. Some he could fit in now. Kent was proving too tough to run off his lands, with too many still-loyal friends. Somebody decided to get rid of him. But just to gun him down would bring on a massive manhunt. Whoever was behind it didn't want that. So they killed him and provided the killer. All neat, everything wrapped up: Kent out of the way for good and his murderer in hand. Skye Fargo swore softly under his breath. He'd been mousetrapped and they had done a damn good job of it, and that made him angrier than the murder charge. The girl, Kent's bride of only a month, was both the key and

34

the biggest riddle. Was she alone in it here, he wondered, his eyes boring into Bloodhound Conley's broad back riding just ahead of him. Did Conley know more than he? Conley had a reputation for honesty, but Fargo had seen other men with good reputations turn bad. Questions were endless now. He needed more facts to fit anything together. A thought flew through his mind and he gave it voice, calling out to the man riding in front of him.

"Sheriff, how come you arrived so conveniently?" he asked.

Conley turned in the saddle, fastened a cold stare on him. "Somebody came to my office and said there might be trouble at the Kent place," he answered.

"Who?" Fargo pressed.

"Never saw him before," Conley said.

"You get his name?" Fargo questioned.

"No, but he said he was a friend of yours and that you were liquored up and feeling mean and there could be trouble," the sheriff said.

Fargo searched the slate eyes. They told him nothing. "What he'd look like, this friend of mine?" he pressed.

"Thin, small mustache, long jaw," the sheriff said. Conley turned his back on him, continued riding ahead, and Fargo swore silently. If Conley were telling the truth, it had been but one more neat piece of the plan, executed with absolute flawlessness. And he hadn't a damn answer for any of it, except his own speculating, and that sure wouldn't be enough, not now, not for Bloodhound Conley. His story, true as it was, kept sounding thinner each time he told it. "Damn, if only I'd kept the letter," Fargo swore under his breath, but he was never one for keeping a lot of pieces of paper cluttering up his pockets.

The dark shapes of buildings appeared ahead. They had reached Pointed Rock and Conley led the way down Main Street. A few men on the street called out questions and Conley clipped answers at them. When he halted in front of the jail, the rope was lifted from about Fargo's neck and he swung out of the saddle. A gun jammed into his ribs at once. "Inside, bastard," someone growled. Angry voices in the distance drifted to him and he glanced down the dark street toward Lily's place, saw the figures streaming out, voices raised. The news had begun to travel fast.

Pushed forward, Fargo moved toward the jail. His glance scanned the building, wooden with a brick foundation and a narrow alleyway running along one side of it. Inside, it was ordinary enough, maybe a little neater and cleaner than most jails. Fargo saw three small cells, each with a high, barred window, behind the front office area where a rolltop desk and a swivel chair provided most of the furniture. A wall case held six carbines.

"Put him in cell one," Conley ordered. "Untie his hands after you've got him inside."

Fargo might have smiled, only he was in no mood for smiling. He rubbed his wrists after the ropes were taken off, watched the deputy clang the door shut. Conley hung his Remington and the holster inside the cabinet with the carbines, he noted. He watched the sheriff turn to his deputies.

"You and Howie go outside, keep them back. I'll be out in a few minutes," Conley ordered, walked toward the cell, his face hard as stone. "You better pray I can keep that mob outside," the sheriff said. "Howard Kent was a damn well-liked man around here." Fargo saw the man's jaw muscles twitch. "And he was a personal friend of mine, Fargo. I'm going to see that you pay for this."

"I don't pay for things I didn't do," Fargo said.

"You going to stick to that dumb story, are you?"

36

the sheriff said. "Go ahead, it's your neck." He spun around, strode to the door, and pulled it open. The roar of sound flooded in at once, an angry, turbulent sound full of shouting voices. It returned to a muffled roar as the door closed. Fargo went to the high window, pulled at the bars, found no give, no weakness in any of them. He turned from the window to scan the front of the jail again. One door out, only a few feet from the rolltop desk and the swivel chair. Two lamps lighted the jail, one atop the desk, the other hanging from the ceiling just above the cell door. Fargo's eyes went to the lock on the cell. No rusted, old piece ready for easy picking. Not in Bloodhound Conley's jail, he thought. Getting out would take finding a chance, a moment to seize.

He sat down on the cot, stared into space, and softly cursed flame hair and an overwhelming beauty. Crystal Kent held the answers and he had to get to her. She was like a fruit that was shiny and beautiful on the outside and inside harbored rottenness. He had to get to her, scare, shake, or beat the truth out of her. Right now it was almost useless to speculate on what had happened. It was like looking at a damn mountain from a distance. You saw the shape of it, the outlines of it, but you couldn't see the face of it, the boulders and trees, the cliffs and passes that made it what it was.

His thoughts broke off as the door opened and Conley entered with one of the deputies. The sound of the mob outside had receded to a low rumble now. "They're cooled off for now," Conley said. "But tomorrow night, when they booze it up again, they'll be back, meaner and madder than now."

"What'd you do with my horse?" Fargo questioned.

"In the stable, not that you'll be using him," the sheriff said, turned to the deputy. "You take tonight," he said, and drew the man aside, spoke to him in low tones. Fargo gave up trying to overhear, sat back on the cot, leaned against the wall. He saw Conley leave and the deputy lock the door. A paunchy man with a heavy stubble, he sat down in the swivel chair for a few moments, put his gun on the desk. He rose abruptly, turned out the lamp that lighted the cells, and lowered the one atop the desk to a tiny flame. The cell was plunged into almost total darkness, and Fargo stretched out on the hard cot. He managed to sleep some, waking every hour to glance at the dim figure of the deputy in the chair. The clock over the rolltop desk, he managed to make out, read 5:00 A.M. when he got to his feet. It was as good a time as any to try a move, the Trailsman decided.

"Hey, deputy," he called out through the dimness, saw the man snap awake. "How about some water? Or is that against the house rules?"

The man swiveled in the chair, peered at the darkened cell for a moment, then took a glass from a shelf, poured from a heavy white pitcher, started toward the cell with the glass in hand. Fargo's eyes flicked to the bars, spaced wide enough to reach through. He lifted on the balls of his feet, dropped one shoulder. He'd have to do it in one smooth instant motion, fasten one hand around the man's throat, the other on his gunhand. He waited but as the deputy neared, the man drew his gun, leveled it at the Trailsman as he passed the glass through the bars. "Just so's you don't get any ideas," he growled.

Fargo eyed the heavy Colt, the barrel aimed at his stomach. He took the glass, drank, handed it back. The gun hadn't wavered an inch. He turned away, cursed silently. Conley had plainly told his men to be extra careful, another backhanded compliment. Fargo lay down on the cot and let the rest of the night drift away in sleep.

He was awake when Conley arrived in the morning, halting in front of the cell as a deputy brought in a bowl of water and a towel. "I sent a rider to fetch Judge Brown," the sheriff said. "He ought to be back tomorrow with him."

"No hurry on my account," Fargo commented as he rinsed his face.

"Smart talk won't save your hide if that mob gets past me tonight," the sheriff said. "It hurts me to have to save your neck."

"But you'll do it," Fargo said.

"Yes, because I've never lost a prisoner, not to a mob or by an escape. Oh, some of them have gotten out, but I brought them back, dead or alive. So you'll stay safe until a judge and jury sentence you," the sheriff said grimly.

"You'll excuse me if I don't seem real grateful," Fargo returned. He saw the sheriff turn away as two more deputies entered the jail. The man busied himself, left after an hour, two deputies remaining inside. Food, two slices of sour-dough bread and a soggy omelette, arrived, one deputy setting the small tray on the cot while the other one trained his gun on Fargo until the cell door was closed again. Fargo ate the food mechanically. They were definitely ordered to take no chances. He had to find a way to make them make a mistake. But they made none when they ordered him to hand the tray and plate out through the bars, and once again Fargo folded himself onto the cot. He let his head hang down, but he peered through slitted eyes at all that went on, deputies changing shifts, Conley returning, leaving again.

Fargo saw the night close around the edges of the barred window and he felt his hands clenching and unclenching, the seething inside him made more of cold rage than fear, frustration more than worry. He had spent the day in a corner of the cell, waiting, watching, trying to spot one chance, one opportunity, but nothing even resembling a gamble had appeared. The night gathered around the jail, grew late, and he forced himself not to think about anything but getting out. First things first. Conley was inside the front office with two more deputies when the sound began to rumble down the street, roll toward the jailhouse, finally taking on definition in the shouts of angry voices.

Conley left one deputy inside, took the other two with him, carbines for each, and stepped outside. Almost instantly, Fargo heard the heavy sound of the rifle firing twice and then the dull roar diminishing, dropping away to a low rumble. He rose, paced the cell, eyed the deputy, a young man with tousled hair, tried to find some excuse to bring him closer. "Cigarette?" he tried. The man turned, started toward him, pulling a cigarette pack from his vest pocket. When he neared, he halted, tossed the cigarette into the cell, followed with the book of matches. Fargo grunted thanks, scooped up the cigarette, and swore to himself. Bloodhound Conley knew all the tricks and he'd briefed his men carefully.

The sound outside rose, dropped away again, and it was over a half hour when the front door opened and Conley came in, holding the carbine in one hand, alone. "They're breaking up," he said to the deputy with a deep rush of breath. "Took some hard talking, though. Judge Brown better get here tomorrow." He shot a glance at Fargo. "He give you any trouble?" he asked the deputy.

"Nope," the man said.

"You go on home, Jake. I'm on tonight," the sheriff said as Fargo, huddled in a corner, watched from beneath lowered eyes. He saw the deputy leave, Conley bolt the door and methodically turn out the cell lamp, then lower the desk one until there was but one small circle of light around the swivel chair. Once again, the cell was in darkness and Fargo sat up, watched the sheriff settle his big form into the swivel chair. The man pushed the chair against the wall, put his carbine over his lap and his head back against the wall. In minutes, Conley was asleep, his breathing filling the silence with a heavy rasping. Fargo stretched out on the cot, his eyes narrowed, stared up at the ceiling. The chance he needed was proving a lot more elusive than he'd expected, thanks to Bloodhound Conley's caution and experience. He lay awake, letting his mind explore possible avenues to try in the morning, dissatisfied with each one that came to mind. The sheriff's heavy breathing filled the silent cell like a rasping dirge, and Fargo's lips pulled back in a silent grimace as he continued to find fault with the thoughts that moved through his consciousness.

He didn't hear the soft steady tapping at first, and then it filtered into his straining thoughts. He sat up at once, every muscle tensed, his ears straining. The tapping sounded almost like the drip of water, but it wasn't steady enough and it was coming from the barred window. Fargo rose to his feet, stood on the cot, moved to the window at eye level. The face materialized out of the darkness, on the other side of the bars, a strong face with high cheekbones and a wide mouth.

Fargo's jaw dropped open in surprise and the girl put her finger to her lips as his breath drew in sharply. He saw she was on a horse as her hand lifted, pushed between the bars, and the dull metal shape caught his eyes. He closed his fingers around hers and took the gun from her hand, pulled it into the cell. "I'll be waiting back of the stable," she said, forming the words soundlessly with her lips. He

41

nodded, watched her move away from the window, out of his line of vision. The big man stepped down from the edge of the cot, landed on the floor on his toes. He looked down at the gun in his hand and half-smiled in the darkness. "Good deeds," he murmured, "sometimes pay off." He stepped to the bars, the gun behind his back.

"Sheriff," he called out. Conley snapped awake instantly, frowned into the darkness. "I want to talk to you," Fargo said. "I want to confess."

He saw the sheriff push forward in the chair, get to his feet, and turn up the kerosene lamp. Light reached out to the edge of the cell and Conley put the carbine down, started to move toward the bars. Fargo waited as the man halted a few feet from him, his eyes boring into him.

"You say you want to confess?" the sheriff echoed. "Just like that? All of a sudden?"

"That's right," Fargo answered.

"You get religion suddenly?" Conley asked, scratched his chin with one hand.

"No, but I got this," Fargo said, bringing the revolver up, aiming it directly at the man. "One move and I'll blow your head off, Conley," he growled, waited as the sheriff's eyes took in the gun, flicked to the distance between himself and the wall. "Don't even think about it," Fargo said softly. "Drop your gun belt, nice and slow."

"You won't get far," the man said as he undid the gun belt, let it slide to the floor.

"Now the keys," Fargo said. "Toss them over here." Conley, fury in the gray eyes, took the keys from his pocket, tossed them, and Fargo saw them land up against the metal edge of the cell door. "Now move over to the wall," he ordered, waited till the sheriff was against the wall before bending down to reach out and pick up the keys. Keeping the gun

42

trained on the man, feeling with his fingers, Fargo pushed the key into the lock, turned it, and the door sprang open. He stepped out, the gun still on the sheriff. "Turn around," he snapped, and Conley obeyed. The Trailsman pulled a kerchief from the man's back pocket, tied it around his mouth. He felt Conley's shoulder muscles tighten, jammed the gun into the small of his back. "I wouldn't try it," he hissed. He backed away, moved backward to the desk, and rummaged through the top drawers until he found a coil of strong twine. He tied Conley's arms behind him, pushed him into the cell, and locked the door. The sheriff, arms bound tightly, the kerchief over his mouth, turned to face him, and Fargo saw the hate in the gray eyes.

"Now I know what you're thinking, Conley, and my running only makes you more convinced," Fargo said. "But I'm going to tell you one more time. I didn't kill Kent. You're just too damned thickheaded to believe me, and I sure as hell can't prove it to you in a cell or hanging from a noose, so I'm cutting out. You find out who really did it instead of chasing after me and you'll be doing the right thing."

He halted, saw the disbelief and rage in the man's eyes that glowered at him over the kerchief. He drew a deep sigh. He'd wasted breath and time, but he had to say it once more. Now he turned, opened the door a fraction to peer out. The streets were empty and he slipped into the night, closing the door quietly behind him. The stable was but a few long loping strides away, and he entered it on cat's feet, saw the pinto in the first stall. He was starting to saddle up when the stableboy appeared, stared at him, uncertainty in his eyes, then fear as Fargo leveled the gun at him. "Sit down and be quiet, boy," he said, and the youth fell back onto a bench against one wall, stayed as if frozen in place. Fargo finished the last hitch, swung into the saddle, and aimed the gun at the boy once more. "Don't move for another ten minutes," he said.

"Yes, sir," the boy replied. "I'm staying right here." Fargo rode from the stable, turned the corner to the rear of it. She was there, waiting, the moon outlining the handsomeness of her strong face.

"We ride now and talk later," Arlene Hargrove said. "I know a place. You'll be safe there, for a day or so at least."

He nodded, and she slapped the horse, took off in a gallop. Fargo sent the pinto after her, pulled up to ride beside her, stride for stride. He watched the way her hair blew behind her in the wind, pulled almost straight back. She could ride, sat her horse damn well. She led the way over low hills, down through narrow gulleys, and over fields of scrub brush. He followed her into a rocky ravine, through another sharp twisting turn, and reined up as she came to a quick stop, a small hut outlined in the dark. She dismounted and he looked down at her.

"Old miner's shack. Almost nobody knows about it. I stay the night here often when I feel like being alone," she said matter-of-factly.

"You often feel like that?" he asked.

"Sometimes," she answered, watching him dismount. "You'll be safe here till you decide what you want to do." She went inside and he watched as she lighted a hurricane lamp and the glow fanned out for him to see a room with a brass bedstand, a fireplace, two chairs, a handful of wooden shelves with jars and dried foods. He moved to stand in front of her, took her shoulders in his hands.

"Thanks," he said simply. "What made you do it? Paying back good deeds?"

44

"That's some of it," the girl said evenly, her eyes holding his.

"What's the rest?"

"I couldn't see you killing Mr. Kent," she told him. "A man who'd come this far to kill Howard Kent wouldn't risk his life to help a girl and her young brother. He wouldn't even stop."

Fargo half-smiled. "You're right. I didn't kill Kent, though you're probably the only one around here who believes me. But I'm going to prove it. I'm going to find out who did it."

"Unless Conley catches you first," Arlene Hargrove said. "Why'd Crystal Kent say you did it?"

"Dammed if I know the answer to that one," Fargo bit out. "I've got to find a way to get to her."

The girl turned from him, gestured to the hut's interior with a wave of her hand. "You can stay here while you think out your plans," she said.

"You going back to the ranch?" he asked.

"Not tonight," she said, turning to him. He saw her hand go to the wool shirt she wore, unbutton the top button, then the second, the third following. She faced him, her eyes watching his face.

"More paying back good deeds?" he asked softly.

"No, I've done that," she answered. "This is for me, because I've done nothing but think about you and hope you might come back this way. You're here, not the way I'd thought about your coming back, but you're here."

He reached out, put a hand around the back of her neck, drew her to him. "And you're hungry," he said.

Her eyes flashed protest. "Not because there was nobody wanting. There were plenty of them," she snapped.

"Yes, I believe that," Fargo told her.

"I don't settle for less than I want," she said.

"How do you decide what you want?"

"Something goes off deep inside. I know then. It's not hard, if you know how to listen to yourself," she said.

He felt the smile come over his face. Just listen to yourself, he thought, so simple, yet a kind of wisdom most people never come to know. Right now he couldn't help but listen to the surge of desire that gathered itself in his loins as she undid the last two buttons of the shirt, pulled it free of her belt. Her breasts came free, firm and young and beautifully shaped, small pink tips that stood out proudly by themselves. Her arms lifted, reached backward, and she shook the shirt from her, her eyes never leaving his. She turned finally, moved to the side of the bed against the wall. He was with her in two long steps, his hands curling around each lovely breast, slowly running his thumbs over each pink tip, feeling them grow firmer, filling with wanting. He bent his head down to each, letting his lips close around first one then the other. It was a beginning and the girl's breath sang out in a long sigh of pleasure.

He undid snaps and buckles, his own and hers, and she moved with him, pressing her mouth against his, pushing her lips upward in welcome. She made love with little sighs, unfettered pleasure, but with a simplicity of the senses, free of all guile, all false coyness, and her body, like her face, was made of angular handsomeness, hips wide and flat, abdomen hardly curved at all. When she turned and twisted in pleasure as his hands caressed the dark and hidden places, she moved with easy grace. There was something deerlike about her, like a young doe that moved with graceful ease and unvarnished beauty.

"Yes, oh, yes, yes," she gasped out as he entered her softness, and her legs came around his buttocks and grew taut as she pressed herself to him and he caught the little smile that held her lips as the moment drew closer and her body began its short swift thrustings until suddenly her legs around him were soft steel and the cry came from her, rising into the air, urging more, words that were only sounds yet unmistakable in their message. She clung to him for a long time, her body slowly unwinding, and finally she lay against him, asleep, like a cat that had been fed and satisfied and curls up to enjoy the sweet aftermath of feeling good.

He found himself napping beside her, finally relaxing enough to sleep, and when he woke, the sun streamed through the lone window of the hut, a yellow blanket across Arlene Hargrove's back and lean rear. He lay unmoving, her body curled against him, letting his mind gather thoughts about the task ahead. First was to get to Crystal Kent. By now Conley would have his posse organized with riders out looking for signs, asking questions. He wasn't one to go racing off widly. He'd pick up leads first, a trail to follow. All of which meant that Conley would be in the area, waiting for his men to develop a lead.

Fargo's thoughts broke off as the girl stirred, lifted her head, and looked at him, her eyes coming awake. "Making plans?" she asked, and he nodded. She half-turned, lay back, stretched, swung out of bed, and went to a basin with cold water to wash her face. When she returned, she was scrubbed and shiny and fully awake, and she settled beside him with the same unvarnished simplicity, that young-doe quality, he had observed earlier. She leaned back against the wall, her breasts proudly erect, holding themselves out almost straight. She looked at the bear-claw scar on his forearm and she reached out and touched it gently, but she asked nothing about it.

"What do you know about Crystal Kent?" he asked her. "Where does she hail from?"

"I can't help you there," Arlene Hargrove said. "I don't get to hear town gossip. Don't want to either."

Fargo nodded and knew there was one person who would hear whatever was said in town. His lips pursed for a moment as he thought about Lily. She hadn't come to see him while he was in jail, but that didn't say much. Maybe Conley had forbidden visitors. Or maybe she just figured she had to live with the sheriff and his power in town and there was no sense in irritating him. His thought returned to Crystal Kent, a frown sliding over his face.

"Penny for your thoughts," he heard the girl say.

"I'm thinking that I might have to get Crystal Kent away from the ranch to throw some fear into her and loosen her tongue. I might have to bring her here," he said.

"When?" the girl asked.

"Not till tonight. I can't move till after dark," he said.

"I'll be gone back by then," she said. "You can do whatever you want with her."

"I just want the truth out of her," Fargo said.

Arlene Hargrove agreed with a single nod of her head. "Dark's a good while away yet," she said, moved away from the wall, sliding her lithe body to him. Her arms came up to his neck.

"Yes, so it is," he said, and kissed her. She pressed backward, pulling him with her, opening her legs and closing them around him. He moved with her, heard her little cry of pleasure. The dark was indeed a good while away.

Later in the day they slept again, and this time, when he woke, the purple of dusk lay over the tall rocks outside. Arelene rose, naked, fixed something to eat, and he studied the free easy grace of her, every movement as unposed as she had been in bed.

She ate opposite him, sitting cross-legged on the bed, and he found himself sorry the night had come. When she dressed, she turned back to him from the doorway. "Maybe you'll be back to see me again," she said. "Sooner than you think."

"Maybe," he said, and got up, went to the door to stand naked beside her.

She reached up, kissed him, the wool shirt a terrible touch against his bare skin after the warm feel of her bare breasts. "It made all the waiting worthwhile," she murmured, opened the door, and hurried outside. She got her horse, swung onto the mount, looked back at him. "Come back if you can. I expect I'll be waiting," she said, turning, spurring the horse into a trot. He closed the door, listened till the sound of the hoofbeats were gone. He had known many such interludes with young women of many stripes. Most faded quickly enough from the mind. Arlene Hargrove would stay, he knew, because she had the touch of the land in her, the sparse, simple handsomeness of the untrammeled land.

He washed and put on clothes, not hurrying, the later the better for his plans. Finally went outside and got the pinto where the horse grazed on bunchgrass. He swung into the saddle and rode slowly out of the little ravine, finding his way under a low moon that twisted the rocks into dark shapes. When the Kent ranch came into view, he circled the buildings, noting the light from the bunkhouse and the sound of the cowhands inside. Only one light came from the main house, at the right side of the house, and he dismounted, walked the horse to the rear door of the low flat-roofed building. Leaving the pinto outside, he pushed gently at the door and it swung open at once to reveal a long dark corridor. He entered, halted for a moment to let his eyes grow used to the darkness inside, then moved down the corridor. He passed the study with the six tall arched windows, the place of murder and deceit. He went past a library, a dining hall. The bedrooms were at the far end of the corridor and he halted at the first one, the door open, the large master bedroom. The room was neat, but there was no one in the big four-poster bed, and he went on to the next room. The door here was half-closed and he peered inside to the smaller single bed. It, too, was empty.

The next room was a guest room and she wasn't in that either. He turned away, irritated. He'd hoped to find her alone. He began to retrace steps along the corridor, toward the light that was a yellow block on the floor as it came from the other end of the house. He made his way to the edge of the open door, peered carefully around the frame, saw the room was a large kitchen. The Indian-Mexican housekeeper was in the kitchen, peeling potatoes, and Fargo felt the frown dig into his forehead. "Where the hell is Crystal Kent?" he murmured, decided to find out fast. He swung into the room and was at the woman's side before she had a chance to move, clapping one hand to her mouth, taking the peeling knife from her with the other. Her eyes were wide with fright as they looked up at him.

"Be quiet. I'm not here to hurt you," he said, waited until he felt the stiffness leave her arms. "Mrs. Kent, where is she?" he asked, took his hand from the woman's mouth. "Where is she?" he repeated with more edge to it.

"Not here," the woman said. "Gone."

"Gone where? Into town?" Fargo asked, keeping his hand closed around the woman's wrist.

The woman shook her head. "No. She just go. She tell nobody anything."

50

"You lying to me?" Fargo questioned. "You lie and I'll come back."

The fear in the woman's flat broad face was real. "No lie, no lie," she said. "She just go, this afternoon. She say can't stay here, too much hurt."

"Just all choked up with grief, was she?" Fargo murmured bitterly. "What she meant was she did her job and pulled out." He stepped back from the woman, moving with the quickness of a puma, and ran for the pinto before the woman had a chance to draw two long breaths. He vaulted into the saddle and raced off into the darkness, turning the horse toward Pointed Rock. When he neared the town, he slowed, halted when the collection of ramshackle buildings came into sight. He pulled up behind a set of the jagged-top rock formations from which the town had gotten its name. He dismounted and looked down at the town and let the hours drag on. He waited and watched the town grow quiet, silent, lights turn off one by one until only the lights of Lily's place glowed. But deep into the night, those, too, went out. He remounted and moved toward the town, taking the horse behind the back of the buildings until he'd reached the tavern. His eyes took in the windows on the second floor and the low roofed overhang easily within reach.

He moved the pinto under the overhang, reached up, and pulled himself onto the wood ledge from the saddle. He crawled along it on hands and knees, staying below the window line, passing a low throaty laugh coming from one window, an unmistakable cry from another, until he reached the last one, Lily's room. The window was half-open at the bottom and he peered in, let his eyes find Lily's form in the bed, a sheet half over her, a nightgown doing its best to cover her large breasts and only partly succeeding. He lifted the window and swung into room, all in

51

one quick motion, was alongside the bed as Lily sat up, blinked her eyes at him, fright turning into surprise.

"Fargo, what the hell are you doing here?" she gasped. "You crazy? Conley's got everybody looking for you."

"I didn't do it, Lily," the Trailsman said.

The woman's mouth turned wry. "I told Conley that, told him I knew you too well," she said.

"He didn't buy it," Fargo said.

"No, he said that was too long back and men change," she answered.

"Forget Conley. What do you know about Crystal Kent? Where'd she come from?"

"I heard talk she hailed from up around the Tetons, way up beyond South Pass where the Tetons get rough," Lily said. "That's a long time away."

"She's lit out and she may be heading back home," Fargo said. "Doesn't that say something, her not even waiting for the funeral as a proper widow ought to do?"

"Not to Conley. She sent him a note saying she was too afraid to stay with you out of jail and she was going to stay with friends and would be back," Lily told him, and Fargo shook his head grimly. Crystal Kent was a lying little bitch, but as smart as she was beautiful. "Forget her," Lily said. "You go after her and Conley will catch up to you, Fargo."

"I'm not carrying around a killing I didn't do for the rest of my days," Fargo said. "I'm going to get her and she's going to tell the truth."

"Be careful, Skye," Lily said, her eyes holding concern. "Conley won't back off, not with his reputation to keep." She reached up, pressed her lips to his. "For good luck," she said.

He patted her rear and turned away, extended one long leg over the windowsill, followed with the other, dropped from the overhang to land lightly on his feet. He waved up at the dim figure in the dark window and hurried to the pinto. He threaded his way carefully behind the buildings again, sent the horse into a gallop only when he was clear of Pointed Rock. The thin pink line of the morning sun cut over the land ahead. As soon as Conley learned he'd visited the ranch looking for the girl, he'd gather his posse together and start after him. Fargo guessed he'd have a day, maybe two, head start. Not much, he reflected, and the lead could shrink fast. Getting his hands on Crystal Kent remained the first order of business. If she were heading back home, she'd have to go north some and then strike west. He continued on. There were a few homesteader places along the way, he remembered. They might have seen her.

He guided the pinto along the edge of a dry creek with good footing. There was only one bright spot in the whole damn picture. It oughtn't to be hard picking up the trail of a strikingly beautiful flame-haired girl traveling alone. He frowned at once. If she was indeed traveling alone. Another question, that. Maybe she'd met friends waiting for her. He felt his jaw muscles tighten. Everything had questions inside questions. He'd fling all of it away except one thing, getting hold of Crystal Kent. He bent forward in the saddle and spurred the pinto on as he saw the weathered house of the first of the homesteader places.

4

The woman was weathered as the old shack of a house behind her and seemed glad for company and the chance to talk. Fargo kept his manner casual as his questions struck pay dirt. "Oh, yes, she came by yesterday, a real stunner, hair like fire," the woman told him. "She stopped because she'd broke a cinch. Bought another one from my husband, paid him for putting it on for her."

"She have any other trouble?" Fargo asked.

"Had a new shoe on one leg of her horse—foreleg, it was—and she had my husband check it for her, but it was fine," the woman recalled aloud. "Left in a hurry when the cinch was put on."

"Yesterday, you said?" Fargo queried.

"Yep. Late afternoon," the woman said as Fargo turned the information in his mind. Had the news of his escape sent her fleeing, he pondered. Or had she intended to leave anyway?

"Why'd you say you're chasin' after her?" the woman asked, cutting into his thoughts.

"Got an important message for her," Fargo said blandly. "Which way did she head?"

"I'd say toward Elkshead, the way she went off," the woman answered.

"Much obliged," Fargo said, wheeled the pinto around, and headed north. "Elkshead," he repeated softly, his eyes narrowed. It figured, if she were heading back to South Pass. Elkshead was a way station, nothing more, but it made one more thing clear. She was taking the Oregon Trail west, and Fargo swore silently. It made his chase even more desperate. The Oregon Trail was no tamed, ordered passage. It was more a vague route than a marked trail, a route of scorching plains and killing mountains, all the savagery of the hostile land and the angry redman. The Oregon Trail swallowed up wagon trains and lone travelers, sparing some but ravishing more. Fargo raced his horse until he reached the way station and turned west, onto the untamed trail. He had to reach Crystal Kent more than ever now. He needed her alive, able to tell the truth, not one more victim of the Oregon Trail or the Arapahos. Only one thing was certain. If he didn't get to her in time, the Oregon Trail would be the Hanging Trail for him. Bloodhound Conley would see to that.

Once riding west on the trail, he slowed his pace. Forcing a horse was for amateurs and those filled with fear. For Crystal Kent, he hoped. He opened the buttons of his shirt, wrapped his kerchief under his hatband as the sun grew hot, burning down on the ground. He guided the pinto to one side, into a long line of tall panic grass. It made for slower riding, but it kept the horse's legs cool. His thoughts returned to the beautiful young woman he pursued. Who was Crystal Kent, he pondered. An unusually beautiful, reformed tavern girl recruited to do a job? A hooker with obligations to pay off? He grimaced. Usually he could spot even the reformed ones, but she'd shown none of that special hardness that seldom leaves them. Yet she was following orders and she'd put his neck into a noose without hesitating. She remained a complete riddle as he slowed, caught sight of a stream. He let the horse drink, stand in the stream for ten minutes while he walked down to the dry soil of the path.

He squatted down, rose, walked a dozen yards, his mouth tight. The soil was too dry, too loose to pick up anything clear. He'd have to keep on, following a hunch. Returning to the pinto, he rode till midafternoon, then found a cluster of pancake rocks with enough scrub for cover, and spread his bedroll, slept until night came. He ate some beef jerky he carried and set out again in the cool of the night, staying close to the center of the trail, where he expected the girl would ride.

He halted a little before dawn, slept some again, and then continued on through the early morning before the sun came down to burn the land again. His eyes moved continuously back and forth, from one side of the ground to the other, seeking, watching, when suddenly he reined to a halt. He swung from the saddle and hurried to a half-circle near a wide boulder to one side of where he rode. Squatting down, he peered at the remains of a small campfire. But the Trailsman's eyes read the scene as though it were a book, seeing what others would overlook, defining words that were made not of letters but of scuffed soil, marks and identations, prints and pebbles. The face of the land spoke to those who understood and could read its ways, and every creature left its signs. Every redman knew that, and some of that gift was in his blood.

His eyes were small and slitted as he peered at the scene. The fire had been put out but not covered over, done by someone in a hurry to leave. He bent low and sniffed the ground. The fire had been out not more than six or so hours. Footprints were difficult to pick up clearly in the dry loose surface soil, but he managed to make out enough to know that there'd been only one person at the fireside, only one set of prints. Small boot size, a small man, someone who moved with short strides. Or a woman. Crystal Kent. He rose, almost certain he had picked up her trail. Almost. He wanted one more piece of proof before allowing himself certainty.

He returned to the pinto to ride on, and as his eyes peered forward to the horizon sky, he knew he'd have his answer soon. A line of dark clouds rolled toward him, coming out of the west. The thunderheads had been rolling over the trail for hours, he estimated. He was actually riding into them and he spurred the pinto on. The sun burned hot through his clothes and he hurried toward the welcome cool of the storm clouds. He rode into the abrupt downpour, taking to cover as the skies opened over him, welcoming the cleansing, cooling rain. Lightning speared the deep-purple sky and the thunder rolled across the flat plains, the ground grew soft quickly, and he let the pinto find his own pace. Thoroughly soaked, but his body cooled and refreshed, he finally emerged from the storm into the wall of sun on the other side.

But the heavy rain was welcome in still another way as he drew to one side, dismounted, and spread his wet clothes on the ground. He allowed himself the luxury of a half hour to rest and let the sun take much of the wetness from his things, then he remounted and went on. But now he rode along the softened, rain-soaked ground with his eyes glued to the soil. Most of the day had gone when he picked up the trail, dismounted to study the prints of a lone rider. The imprint of a single, crisp-edged, new horseshoe was clear in the rain-softened earth, the left foreleg of the horse, the print deeper, sharper than those of the other three horseshoes.

He stood up, a hard smile touching his lips. That final piece of certainty was his, and he remounted and set off again. She was continuing to ride fast, push her horse, he noted, but she'd have to slow soon. His eyes looked backward for a long moment, scanning the distant horizon. The storm clouds had gone out of sight, but back there, somewhere, Bloodhound Conley followed, doggedly, persistently, gaining ground little by little. He'd have questioned the homesteaders and picked up his trail. Conley surely had a posse and he'd send outriders and flankers out to make certain his quarry didn't cut off, change direction, or double back. It was an advantage that let him make better time, and Fargo felt his lips press together. He turned his eyes back to the trail ahead. He didn't have to see signs to know that Bloodhound Conley was there, inching toward him. It was a grim race with the hunter the hunted.

Fargo cast an eye at the late-afternoon sky, guessed he had a little more than an hour or two before night. He'd bed down in the night now, take no chances on losing the trail now that he had it firmly in hand. Crystal Kent was riding hard and he had no certainty she might not cut off someplace. He couldn't afford to miss that by following at night and he pushed the pinto for a while longer, suddenly very conscious of the unseen presence following behind him.

The long shadows were spreading over the land as he crested a small rise, halted for a moment, and let his eyes scan the terrain on all sides and behind, slowly turning in the saddle. He froze suddenly, frowned, squinted across at a line of low hillocks in the distance. The smudge of dust rose into the air and he watched it move, become horsemen, barely visible. He strained his eyes, counted three of them, riding hard, behind and to his left. He pressed his heels into the side of the pinto and the horse set off at once. He rode, casting frequent glances at the distant horsemen. They were catching up, coming almost abreast of him now but still far across from him. They rode single file, close on each other's heels. Not Indians, he thought. Riding strung out, Indians always kept more distance between their horses.

Conley's men? He winced at the question. Damn, it wasn't impossible. Conley may have sent a trio out to ride as fast and as hard as they could to see if they could spot him while he and the rest of the posse doggedly rode trail. Fargo frowned across the distance at the riders. He was reasonably certain they hadn't spotted him by the way they were riding. And the night would be over the land in less than a half hour. He squinted ahead to where the plains stretched out, wide, dry, only an occasional clump of trees and barren rock formations jutting up as though they'd been dropped there by some giant hand. These were the killing plains, the scorched, burning, shadeless prairies that shriveled and baked the slow wagon trains. By morning the sun would sear man and land again.

He bent forward in his saddle, rode at a slow trot to stir up little dust. The ground was quickly drying out again and he circled behind a cluster of pinnacled rock formations, halted at the far end where they trailed off into a series of broken spires with space in between them: a perfect place for spending the night, protected from wind and prying eyes. He dismounted, disdained making a fire, and let the pinto roam to feed on brush grasses. His body felt the strain of hard riding, the tension of constant searching; and he was grateful for the sleep that came quickly, but not before he wondered again about the three horsemen. It seemed unlikely they could be Conley's men, even riding relentlessly. Yet he had to wonder and only sleep closed off his thoughts.

He woke with the dawn, anxious to move on. He used a little of his water from the canteen to wash, called over the pinto, and had just flung the saddle on the pinto when the voice cut into the silence. "You won't be needing that, mister," it said.

Fargo didn't move, his right hand resting atop the saddle. He heard the click of a pistol hammer. "Turn around, nice and slow," the voice said, and Fargo obeyed, swearing inwardly. The voice became a face, peering down at him from one of the pinnacled rocks, an ordinary face under a dirty gray ten-gallon hat. The Colt in the man's hand was aimed at his chest and Fargo saw the other two appear from behind another of the sharp craggy rocks. One wore a grin, wide as though he'd found gold, the other expressionless. "The three horsemen," Fargo muttered.

"Drop your gun," the grinning one ordered. Fargo did as he was told and watched the first one come down from the top of the rock. "Well, now, it looks like you're all finished chasin' after the little lady," the grinning one said.

"Where's Conley?" Fargo asked.

"The sheriff? Don't know exactly," the man said. His grin stayed, Fargo noted, a fixed part of his face, it seemed. Fargo watched the man eye the hand-tooled Mexican leather saddle resting atop the pinto, walk to it. "Jeez, look at this," the man said, his grin widening.

Fargo's eyes moved to the sharp rocks, the spiraled formation, and the opening nearby. It led into the craggy rocks honeycombed with narrow passages. He measured distances and heard the man at the saddle murmur in awe. "I always wanted a saddle like this," the man said, stroking the leather. "This is somethin' special."

"Later. We take care of him first," the one with the dirty hat answered. Both men glanced at the saddle, and Fargo slid his feet sideways. The one with the expressionless face peered around the edge of the rocks, frowned into the distance. "Come on, we're wasting time," the third one called. He peered into the distance again.

"Didn't Conley tell you to keep me alive till he got here?" Fargo asked.

The grinning one turned, cast a quick glance at the other two, and Fargo shifted another inch closer to the opening. "Didn't say anything to us about keeping you alive," the man drawled, and the trio exchanged glances again. Fargo felt the frown slide across his forehead, the stab of suspicion dig into him.

"Conley didn't say anything to you?" he asked. The grinning one continued his inane grin and glanced at the other two again. The stab of suspicion ballooned, took on a sudden realization. "You're not Conley's men at all," Fargo said.

"Now you're getting real smart," the dirty-hat one said with a mirthless chuckle.

Fargo felt the frown dig deeper into his brow. "You're with her," he said. "With Crystal Kent."

"Somethin' like that," the other answered. Fargo turned the cryptic remark over in his mind, leaving more unsaid than said. "When we heard you broke out we'd figured you'd be taking after her."

"So you came looking," Fargo said, moved another inch to the side.

"The boss wouldn't want her in your hands," the grinning one said.

"Of course not. I'd get the truth out of her," Fargo bit out.

"If you held on to her," the man answered. "The boss has got others out looking."

61

"For me?" Fargo asked.

The man's face filled with sly secrecy. "They're out looking," he repeated, cast another quick glance at the other two. Fargo moved sideways a fraction more. The opening was within range now. "Let's get rid of him," the dirty hat said. Fargo measured the distance a final moment, saw the trio exchange glances again, and he seized the split second. He catapulted his body sideways, twisting, diving into the opening behind the rock. He heard the shout of surprise as he hit the ground behind the rock, the shot reverberating in the small space as he rolled, came up on his feet, and raced down the narrow passageway.

"Get him," he heard one of the men shout as he spun into a second passageway branching off from the first. An incline let him climb up toward a narrow ledge of rock hanging out. He leaped, pulled himself up onto the ledge, slid sideways on the narrow surface, and flattened himself down. He heard his pursuers racing down the passageway, past where he had turned into the joining passage. The rock formation wasn't large enough to hide out for long. They'd ferret him out in a matter of minutes and he heard their shouts, then footsteps, one of the men returning to check out the passage he'd taken. They had his Remington, but Fargo stretched a hand down to his leg, at the boot top, pulled out the throwing knife he had strapped there.

He edged forward, enough to peer over the ledge. It was the grinning face that carefully probed into the passage, gun in hand. Fargo pressed his feet against the back of the ledge where the rock rose, took a firm grip on the knife handle. He could hear the other two scrambling along the spiraled rocks nearby. He would have only one chance. It had to be in one quick strike, even ten seconds of fighting would bring the others before he was ready. He pushed forward on his stomach. The man's steps echoed in the narrow passageway and Fargo waited, listened as the steps approached, came under the ledge. He pressed his feet hard against the rock, pushed, propelled himself forward off the ledge. The grinning face started to half-turn, look up as the figure shot from the ledge over his head. He had time only to see the knife blade hurtling down at him as Fargo dropped from the ledge. He tried to twist away, but the blade buried itself at the base of his throat, a tiny fountain of red spurting upward.

He went down, the Trailsman atop him, his body breaking the fall. Fargo saw the grin fade from his face as he dropped the gun in his hand, his eyes glazing over as he tried to halt the flow of red from his throat. Fargo yanked the blade free and the flow became a gusher. The man made a soft gurgling sound and lay still. Fargo pushed himself up, whirled just as the second figure appeared at the end of the passageway. Fargo scooped up the gun lying beside the dead man's fingers, fired a single shot before the other man could bring his gun up. The figure shuddered, fell backward out of his sight, and Fargo pushed himself to his feet, heard the guttural groan. He ran to the end of the passage. The second one lay with his knees drawn up, face contorted in pain, a pool of red on the ground beside his stomach.

The shot came from above, sent pieces of rock flying a fraction of an inch from his head, and Fargo dropped on all fours, rolled as the second shot slammed into the rock where he'd been. Using his legs, he pushed himself back just inside the passageway as a third shot creased his jacket. He lay unmoving, holding his breath. The wait seemed hours when it was really only moments, and finally he heard the scrape of boots on the pinnacled rocks above. The man was coming down, making his way carefully. Fargo continued to remain absolutely still as the footsteps scraped down farther. His hand lifted, positioned the gun, his finger resting firmly on the trigger. He heard the man drop to the ground, move carefully toward the passageway, come into view, gun ready. But it took a split second for him to focus on the form lying on the ground. Fargo fired during that instant, saw the shot hit the man full in the chest. The dirty hat flew from his head as he arched backward. Fargo rolled over as the answering shot, fired as the gunman fell, slammed into the ground. He swung back, ready to fire again, but the gunman lay spread-eagled, chest shattered by the shot.

Fargo got to his feet, looked down at the man, saw that death had already staked its claim. He made a face, bent down, and went through the man's pockets, then did the same with the other two. He found nothing to answer any of the questions that revolved in his head, and he retrieved his knife, wiped it clean, and put it back in the leg strap. He took his Remington back and stood up, let his eyes move out beyond the rock formation to the horizon, returned his gaze to the three dead men. Their remarks danced in his head, unfinished, cryptic words. Others were looking. For him? For Crystal Kent? To help her to safety? Or to silence her forever? Only one thing had come out of it. The pack was growing. Bloodhound Conley and his posse weren't the only ones seeking him.

He turned, strode to the pinto, and finished where he'd left off, tightening the saddle and bridling the horse. He mounted, moved away from the rocks. The three horses were tied a dozen yards away behind the highest of the rocks. He left them there for Bloodhound Conley to find when he finally came along. He wouldn't be able to just pass by. He'd have to stop and see what the horses meant. Fargo nodded in satisfaction to himself. It would cancel out the delay he had experienced. He touched the pinto on the rump and the horse trotted out once again onto the dry parched prairie.

Fargo looked behind as he rose, eyes squinting to the distant horizon. There were no spirals of dust and his glance swept both sides of the land, saw nothing on either side. He rode on under a sun that had already begun to coat the land with heat waves that made distant objects shimmer and grow wavy. He rode steadily, eyes as much on the ground as searching distances. It was just past midday when he halted, peered down at the trail of hoofprints that moved at an angle, the unshod hooves of Indian ponies. He followed their path: they rode single file, curved to the left, then swung back again. He returned to his own path, picked up the Indian prints again. They had ridden a path paralleling his own and he felt a push of uneasiness as his glance swept the prairie. "No hiding place," he muttered, "distant hills too far away to help." He scanned the prints again. A small party, yet big enough to be hunting buffalo. Or settlers.

He'd gone only a few miles farther when he had his answer. He first saw the charred framework of the lone wagon, only the metal frame under the canvas still standing, tilting into the wisps of smoke that rose up from the base. He rode forward toward the remains. One wagon only, he noted, his lips tightening. One wagon of damnfools. He halted at the scene. A man lay draped over the remains of the wagon, his scalp missing. Fargo's eyes found the woman a few yards away on the ground, more naked than not, legs raised upward and covered with streaks of blood. Terror and agony still held her lifeless face under the brown hair matted with blood. His eyes continued to search, found the two smaller bodies, two girls, nine or ten perhaps. It was hard to tell. They had become women and corpses all in one short moment.

He turned away under the wings of the buzzards that wheeled in slow circles, dipping ever lower. He couldn't take the time to bury the victims and he hoped Conley would let two of his men do it and catch up later. Fargo, cursing human stupidity, started to ride off but reined up shortly, his glance catching sight of the object on the ground. He dropped from the pinto and picked up the piece of rawhide armband with the beadwork around it. His eyes studied the pattern of the armband, symmetrical lines crossing each other in bands of red and yellow beads with a thin line of green. He grunted, the pattern unmistakable. Arapaho. He climbed back onto the pinto, threw the armband on the ground, and galloped off. The small party had been more than enough for a lone wagon. If the Arapaho came upon Crystal Kent with her flame-red hair, she'd never answer questions for anyone again. Her brilliant tresses would be the prize on any tepee wall. Fargo spurred the pinto on, his jaw set tight. Behind him, he knew, Bloodhound Conley rode at the head of his posse, steadily, inexorably closing the distance between them, his slate-gray eyes filled with cold promise.

The Trailsman picked up Crystal Kent's trail with ease. He was definitely drawing closer to her, the new hoofmark of her horse clearer and sharper. She wasn't making as good time either. He found two spots where she'd stopped to rest and the horse had gone into a definitely shorter stride, a sure sign of tiredness. He found a small waterhole where she had stopped, dismounted, her boot prints at the water's edge. He leaned down almost double in the saddle, let one long arm reach down to one of the footprints, his fingers pressing into the firmness of the mark. Twenty-four hours, he told himself as he straightened up. Another twenty-four hours, maybe a little less, and he'd have her. Yet a hell of a lot could happen in twenty-four hours. He glanced backward as far as he could see. There was nothing there, but Bloodhound Conley was back there someplace. Yet not too close. There was still time to reach Crystal Kent first. Fargo spurred the pinto on.

The girl was holding to a fairly straight line across the scorched plains and it was a few hours later when Fargo reined to a halt, frowned down at another set of unshod pony tracks. They crossed his path, moving northward in a slow circle. He guessed maybe fifteen or so riders from the hoofprints and let the pinto follow the tracks for a while to see if they continued north. Suddenly he halted, stared at the marks covering the ground. The new band had joined up with the other one. Twenty-five, maybe thirty Arapaho now, no small party out for lone wagons any longer. The combined tracks continued north in the long circle, and he turned away. He hadn't time to follow any longer and he returned to his own tracking, aware that the Indian band could have circled back at any time.

He didn't like the feel of it, the smell of it, the odds that were beginning to tilt away from him. Conley behind him, God knows who else out looking for him or the girl, a sizable band of Arapaho in the area, and Crystal Kent still twenty-four hours away. The twenty-four hours were looking smaller and smaller. He rode on until night came, tied the pinto to a small clump of scrub trees, unsaddled the horse, and ate without a campfire. He lay atop the bedroll and slept at once, his body grateful for the rest.

He woke an hour before dawn and was riding before the day began to spread over the land. He picked up her trail again and rode hard as the sun climbed higher into the sky. He'd gained at least one hour, maybe two on her, he guessed. He needed every moment. Bloodhound Conley was still back there, still following, the relentless pursuer. Fargo continued to ride at a steady pace, and it was almost the middle of the afternoon when he saw land begin to rise, grow less parched, the grass deeper. Within the hour he saw the hills that rose in front of him, cutting across the plains like a high fold across the center of a bed sheet. The land rose in a series of small but steep hills, heavy brush and tree cover on some of them and steep sides of dirt on the others. The sharp slanted hills formed a series of V-shaped little pockets between them.

Crystal Kent's trail led up into the sharp hills, and he followed, suddenly pulling back, wheeling his horse behind a tall boulder. A handful of riders crossed a ridge in the far distance, riding east along the edge of the farthest hills. He counted from behind the boulder, six in all. No settlers headed west, too far ahead to be Conley's men, and they were no band of idle cowhands returning from a drive, not out here. He watched the riders as they headed down the other side of the steep-sided hill, glimpsed them move south on the flatland, stayed back until they had disappeared from sight.

He moved from behind the boulder and continued on into the steep hills as night descended. He halted, rested his horse and himself for an hour, then rose to walk the horse carefully up the first steep hill to the top. He rested there, peered down into the V-shaped pocket formed by the hills, letting his

68

eyes move slowly across the bottom of the pocket, searching the blackness. Satisfied, he moved on to another ridge and halted there to again peer down into the deep black of the land at the bottom. He moved in and he had just climbed onto the fourth of the ridges when he dropped to one knee, eyes narrowing as he scanned the dark below. The faint glow of a small fire flickered at the bottom of the V-shaped pocket. He let his eyes adjust to the distance and the flickering glow. A figure moved beside the glow, almost a sihouette, but the outline of long, full hair moved as the figure bent down to the fire. Skye Fargo allowed himself a tight fleeting smile. His chase had come to an end.

Carefully, Fargo began to move down the other side of the ridge, pulling the pinto behind him. He took it slow, silently, watched her form take shape, and saw the horse standing but a few yards from the small fire. She was pouring beans into a skillet as he crept downward. He reached the halfway point of the hill and halted. The rest became too steep for the pinto, almost too steep for him alone, and he eyed the few scraggly brush growths on an otherwise almost smooth, steep surface. He draped the horse's reins over a half-dead mound of scrub brush and lowered himself to the ground, turned on his side, and pressed the steep incline with one foot. The dirt seemed firm enough and he reached one long arm out to grasp hold of a piece of brush, began to lower himself down the steep side. He moved slowly, holding on to the brush as long as he could, then letting go and digging his fingers into the earth. He slowed his slide, moved his grip down six inches, let his body follow. He had to get close to her before she knew he was there or she'd race for the horse. She might even have a gun, he realized. Crystal Kent was still a very unknown quantity.

Flylike, he moved his hands again, let himself slide lower, and dug fingers into the earth to hold himself back. He halted to peer down at the small yellow circle of light. She was intent on getting the skillet on the fire, and once again he used his finger grip to inch downward. He let his legs lower themselves, held with one hand, and found a new spot to dig in with his fingers. But suddenly his fingers slipped away, the soil a bare covering over rock. He clawed quickly at another place, felt himself slipping, but once again the soil lay loosely over rock. "Damn," he whispered as he felt himself sliding down. He used both hands to claw frantically again, but the soil had become a light cover and his fingers dug helplessly against the rock underneath. His slide quickened, plunged out of control in seconds. He twisted his body, tried to grab at a piece of scrub brush, caught hold of an end only to have his weight tear it loose. He was plummeting now, the incline sheer rock, and he glimpsed the girl standing, looking up as he plunged toward her.

He hit bottom and felt the sharp searing pain explode in his ankle as he bounced, fell forward, glimpsed Crystal Kent's wide-eyed face watching him. He rolled, grimaced in pain, tried to grab for her, his hand catching hold of her leg. He saw her seize the skillet, bring it around in a sharp arc, and he twisted away but not before the hot edge of it slammed into his shoulder. He kept rolling, the pain in his ankle excruciating, trying to avoid another blow from the skillet. But the girl was running, the skillet spilled on the ground facedown. Fargo tried to get to his feet, pitched forward as his ankle gave way under him, looked up to see Crystal Kent leaping into the saddle. The horse reared up and she clung, flame hair streaming out behind her. The horse came down and she sent it roaring into the darkness.

Fargo drew the Remington, fired a shot after her, sending it wide and hoping it might bring her to a halt. But his only answer was the pounding of hooves. "Come back here, damn you," he shouted, the cry a gesture to his frustration. He holstered the gun, tried to get up, and fell back in pain. The ankle throbbed and he felt it swelling inside his boot. He moved it gingerly, groaned with the pain, decided there was nothing broken and it was better kept inside the boot. He pulled himself to his feet, fought down the pain, and leaned back against the smooth rock incline. He put as much weight on the ankle as he could and knew he had to walk on it to stop it from stiffening up altogether. He glanced up to where the pinto stood high above. Climbing back was impossible. He'd have to hobble all the way to the end of the incline, where it lowered, then back to retrieve the pinto.

He drew a deep breath, began the task leaning with one hand against the rock, each step on the swollen torn ankle an excruciating one. He was perspiring heavily before he'd gone a half-dozen yards and he cursed at the pain that kept his pace slow as a damn mud snail. He found he had to sink down and rest the ankle every ten minutes, and when he finally began the climb back along the ridge toward the pinto, two hours had passed. It took another hour to make his way up the ridge line to the top, but finally, sinking down to the ground, he could look down to where he'd left the pinto.

"All right now, up here," he called. The horse lifted its head, backed from the branch, felt the tug of the reins, and halted. "Come on, it's all right. Come on, boy," Fargo called. The pinto backed again, tugged harder, and the reins came free. Fargo

71

pulled himself to his feet again as the horse cautiously made its way back along the narrow pathway along the incline. He grasped hold of the saddle horn as the pinto came up to him, got one foot in the stirrup, and pulled himself up onto the saddle. He drew a deep breath, wiped perspiration from his face, let his eyes scan the night. In the distance the sky was beginning to lighten, and below, the fire had burned itself out. The ankle hurt, throbbing heavily, but there was no stiffness in it. Fargo slid his foot into the other stirrup and sent the pinto down the ridge line at a fast canter.

His lips were a thin line as he rode down from the line of small steep hills. Crystal Kent had four hours on him again, but she had a very tired horse and she'd fled in panic. She'd be doing much more slowly by now. He kept the pinto at a steady pace as the hills came to a halt and the flat prairie took over again. The new day spread gray light over the plains, then the sun turned them yellow. Fargo picked up her trail again, heading due west. The horse pulled his stride even shorter and was tiring fast, Fargo noted. He slowed as he crossed a wide train of tracks, unshod hoofprints. The Arapaho party had circled back, crossed over to head east. They had made a lazy S, he saw. He cast a glance around him, scanning the flat prairie, but nothing met his eyes. He didn't bother looking back. Bloodhound Conley would make good use of the four hours he had given him.

He pressed on, picking up her trail at every soft place in the ground. She was pushing her horse too hard. The hoofprints grew deeper every mile, a sign that the horse was coming down heavily with each stride in weariness. He couldn't keep the pace much longer, Fargo knew.

It was almost noon when the Trailsman's eyes

picked up the wagon train, a quarter mile to his left, moving slowly, ponderously over the flat plains. When he came abreast of the distant wagons, he counted six Conestogas and two supply wagons, a dozen extra horses strung out behind on a long tether. He thought of the Arapaho band at once, plenty big enough now to attack more than a lone wagon. Turning off to warn the wagon train would lose still more time for him, he thought. Besides, the Indians had passed two hours back at least, heading in the other direction. He rode on, leaving the distant wagons behind.

He'd gone perhaps another half-mile when he reined to a halt, frowned down at the trail. He'd picked up no hoofprints at all, not for at least a half-mile, and he wheeled the pinto around, slowly retraced his steps, searching the ground again. He let his eyes move to each side, found nothing. No hoofprints at all. He continued back to where he'd seen the last mark, dismounted, and pressed his hand down into the hoofprint. It was fresh, very fresh. He moved forward again and found nothing further, turned back, scanned the heavier, thicker yellowed grass that grew out from the center of the trail. It was too heavy to pick up a trail and she just might have cut off across the plains, but he made a face at the thought. It made no sense. There was no place to go, no place to hide. The beginning of mountain country and the Sweetwater River lay directly ahead and that's where she was plainly headed.

He climbed into the saddle, frowning. "No damn place to hide," he repeated, "no place to cut off to here." His gaze wandered out across the flatlands. The wagon train plodded slowly on in the distance. Suddenly his frown dug into his brow. "Shit," he exploded. There damn well was someplace to hide. He stared at the distant wagons, let his gaze flick to the heavy grass, back to the wagons again, the answer taking shape in his thoughts. She knew he was following now, of course, and she'd dismounted, walked her horse across the thick grass to the wagon train. That's why her tracks simply disappeared. "Damn," he swore under his breath. She'd of course readied some sort of story for them to get both sympathy and cooperation. Fargo, biting down on his lips, spurred the pinto across the flatlands toward the wagons.

He reached the train at a canter and moved up to the lead wagon, driven by a man with a full gray beard and wearing a flat-brimmed hat. A woman of ample proportions sat beside him, cradling a single-shot Hawkens Brothers plains rifle in her lap. Fargo raised a hand in greeting and the man pulled back on the reins, brought the wagon to a halt.

"'Afternoon," Fargo said, staying in the saddle. "You the leader of this train?"

The man nodded gravely, sizing up the black-haired man with the piercing blue eyes. "I am," he said. "Moses Adamson. Can we help you?"

"Maybe," Fargo said evenly. "Did you see a young woman ride this way? She'd be alone, a head of bright-red hair."

"This is no land for a woman to ride alone," the man said, not changing his expression. "Nor for anybody."

"True enough, but she'd be alone," Fargo said.

"What do you want with her?" asked the man carefully.

"Got a message for her," Fargo answered.

The man's expression was one of careful control. "Sorry, can't help you any," he said. Fargo glanced at the woman. Her face was equally set.

"She'd have passed you," Fargo said.

"Maybe too far off for us to see," the man said. His face stayed as though set in stone. He was lying,

74

Fargo knew. The woman's face was equally controlled.

"Maybe," Fargo said. He backed the pinto a few paces. "Where you heading?" he asked casually.

"Oregon," the man said.

"Sorry to have bothered you."

The man snapped the reins and the big Conestoga began to roll again, the others following behind. Fargo moved down past the line, taking in young couples, families with kids, older people, the usual mix of dreamers and hopefuls. He let the wagons go by, waited for the line of extra horses to reach him. He moved the pinto closer as they came up, focusing on each one. He reached out, let his hand touch the back of each horse as it passed. The last one came past and his eyes glinted. He ran his hand along the horse's back to confirm what he'd already spotted. The horse's hide was wet, the remains of heavy lather still clinging to the hair, the only one of the extra horses not dusty and dry to the touch.

He swung the pinto away and rode off. He went on ahead, outdistancing the wagons, keeping on till he was out of sight, his eyes ice-blue. He rode almost to where the land began to change character, the flat plains ending, hills and forest taking shape and beyond them, the high mountains. He halted just behind a low rise, dismounted and lay down on his stomach, squinting back along the prairie. She'd stay with the wagon train while they were on the plains, he figured, aware he'd be prowling back and forth looking for her. He settled down and waited, and the day was nearing an end when the wagon train came into sight. He watched it roll closer, finally halt to make camp for the night while still on flatland. His glance shifted past the wagons to the dim horizon, an automatic gesture now. He didn't expect Bloodhound Conley yet, but the delays were

75

helping to bring him close. "Too close," Fargo muttered. He could almost feel the man's presence, and his jaw tightened as he watched the wagons form a half-circle for the night. Figures poured out of the big Conestogas, children, men, and women, most moving purposefully at one or another task. He was beginning to wonder if he'd made a mistake about her staying with the train when suddenly he saw her, swinging down from the last wagon, a brilliant flash of red.

He saw her seek out Moses Adamson, exchange words with the man, lean one hand on his arm for a moment. "Beautiful little bitch," Fargo muttered. She was playing her role to the hilt, whatever story she'd concocted for the man. He watched as she helped gather wood for the campfire, and he shifted his position as the darkness pulled itself over the last of the daylight. He waited patiently, eyes following every move of the girl's as supper was cooked and eaten, the dishes cleaned, and the fire banked low. The children crept into the wagons to sleep, then the adults followed. Fargo watched Crystal Kent as she finally climbed into the last wagon, following a white-bearded man, an elderly woman, and a young couple. A few minutes later the young couple came out to spread a bedroll under the wagon. They laid their heads down toward the front wheels, Fargo noted carefully. He let the night deepen until the fire had all but burned down, the camp a silent, sleeping place.

He rose, took the pinto's reins, moved on foot down toward the camp, circling back of the wagons, halting first at the extra horses tethered together. He cut out the one Crystal Kent had been riding, looked at the animal's feet. The horse had rested, its feet in good shape, he saw, and he took a saddle from the supply wagon nearby, placed it on the horse, and secured it. He led both horses to the back of the Conestoga where the girl slept, sidling near the wagon from the rear, away from the heads of the young couple sleeping underneath. Taking his kerchief out, he made a small ball of it and climbed through the back of the Conestoga, saw her at once, sleeping against one side of the wagon, the old couple bedded down at the opposite side. He crept to her, taking the Remington from its holster. Bending over her, he saw her clothes and a small traveling bag beside her, pushed everything close to his feet. She slept with lips slightly parted, beautiful even in the almost total darkness, the slow rise of one breast coming out of the nightdress she wore.

Moving with one swift motion, he jammed the kerchief into her mouth and put the gun barrel against her temple. She snapped awake, but the kerchief stifled her cry. Her eyes widened in fright as she saw him and the gun pressed to her temple. "Make one sound and this'll go off. I'm very nervous," he whispered. "Understand?" She nodded, eyes round. "Take your things," he ordered, moved to let her sit up. He kept the gun at her temple, the other hand against the kerchief in her mouth as she gathered her clothes and bedroll. She swept up a canteen and he moved with her as she stretched her legs out, started to clamber from the wagon. Once outside, he cast a quick glance under the frame of the Conestoga. The young couple were still hard asleep and he pushed Crystal Kent to where the horses waited. "Into the saddle," he hissed, poking the gun into her back.

She climbed onto her horse, the nightgown pulling, her breasts almost pushing up out of the garment, full, creamy mounds. She wriggled her shoulders, freed the gown to rise up higher, and he reached up, took the kerchief from her mouth. "No

77

funny business," he warned as he swung into the saddle. He took the reins from her hand, walked the horse behind the pinto, keeping the Remington pointed at her. He saw her eyes take in the gun, discard any thought of fleeing. Fargo walked a half-dozen yards from the wagon, then fell back a pace and brought his hand down hard on the horse's rump. The animal shot forward, galloping hard in seconds, and Fargo sent the pinto after her.

He came up alongside her, reached out, and took the reins from her hands. She pulled back and he decided they'd make better time with her doing her own riding. "Straight ahead," he said, riding for the first of the low hills. He kept on over the ridge line and down the other side, deeper into the rich, green forest land. He slowed the horses to a steady pace and led the way along a small trail, past a line of hackberries and higher into the mountain country. The pink of the new day had come to settle in the sky when he halted in a small clearing. "We rest a spell here," he said, and watched her slide from the horse, the nightgown pulling up to reveal lovely legs, softly turned thighs, full of flesh yet firm. Her beauty wasn't all in her face and flame-red hair.

"I'm cold. I want to dress," she said, turning to him, quiet fury in her brown eyes.

"Go ahead," he said casually as he dismounted.

"Turn your back," she said.

He grunted wryly. "Try again," he said.

"I'm not putting on any shows," she snapped.

"That's a pretty thick tree trunk there." He pointed. She threw an angry glance at him, swept up her things, and strode off behind a big oak. He caught flashes of arms and legs as she pulled the nightgown off and dressed, and he had the thought of stepping to the tree to watch her. He put it aside. He wanted her cooperation, not her fury, now. She stepped out in a few minutes wearing a dark-green shirt and black jodhpurs, running her hands through her hair, shaking it vigorously. The new sun caught the fire of it to send little sparks of brilliance into the morning. Her breasts held the green shirt out boldly and she went to her canteen, freshened her face with water from it, finally turned to face him.

"What do you want with me?" she asked coolly.

"You damn well know what I want," he shot back. She met his eyes with almost insolent coolness. "I want the truth out of you," he said.

She looked away, turning her classically beautiful profile to him in dismissal. "I've said all I'm going to say," she remarked.

He felt the surge of anger shoot through him, grabbed her arm, and whirled her around. "God-dammit, you're going to tell me the truth and then you'll tell it to Conley," he shouted.

She tried to pull away, found she couldn't. "You're hurting me," she said, still cool.

He released her arm and took her chin in his hand, lifted her face without gentleness. "You're going to tell me what this is all about," he growled. "Then you're going to tell the truth to Conley. Now, you can do it the easy way by being smart, or you can make me beat it out of you. If I have to do it that way, I will."

"No, you won't," she said through lips hardly opened.

He let her chin go, his eyes hardening. "The hell I won't. You're not sticking that killing on me, beautiful."

Crystal Kent's coolness returned. "You beat it out of me and that's exactly what I'll tell Conley when you bring me to him. I'll tell him you beat me to make me say you didn't do it," she told him.

Fargo felt his hands clench as he glared at her. She

79

glared back, no fear in her at all, he saw. She'd thrown out no hollow threat, he realized. If he took her to Conley, she'd do exactly that: retract her story and scream he'd beaten her to say it. He'd be back in the same spot and in Conley's hands again. He saw the quiet triumph, a smugness, form in her eyes.

"Figure it as a Chinese standoff, do you?" he slid at her. The small half-shrug of her shoulders answered him. "Well, you can guess again. I'll keep you up in these mountains all damn winter till you tell me the truth and agree to stick by it," he said.

"No. You can't," she blurted. The alarm had leaped into her eyes, an instant reaction. He'd touched something.

"I sure as hell can and I sure as hell will," he answered. "So you can start talking, now."

He saw her cover the alarm in her eyes at once with a sullen anger. "Go to hell," she said.

It was his turn to half-shrug. "Suit yourself," he said. He let his eyes move slowly over her face down across the broadness of her shoulders, linger on the twin points pushing out the shirt. He examined her slowly, deliberately, letting her follow his eyes. "It might just be a damn enjoyable winter," he murmured quietly. He lifted his eyes to hers, saw the seething fury inside them, and turned away. But he had seen that instant of panic and he'd bear down on it. He had hold of her and that was the most important thing. He'd find the way to get the truth out of her and he hadn't completely set aside fanning her hide if necessary.

He stepped onto a ledge of stone and gazed down over the flat plains they'd just left behind. The wagon train wasn't in sight yet, but it would be plodding along soon. Moses Adamson was no doubt wondering why the young woman had fled in the night. Fargo's eyes went across the distant horizon and he swore under his breath. Bloodhound Conley was less than a day back now, he guessed, perhaps as little as twelve hours. He stepped from the rock, silently cursing all the delays. "Mount up," he snappd to Crystal Kent.

"Where are we going? she asked truculently.

"Wandering," he bit out. "Better get used to it. You'll be doing a lot of it unless you start talking."

She turned away, but not before he'd caught the glint of panic touching her eyes again, her lips compressing for an instant. He started up the narrow trail bordering the oaks on one side, a view of the land just below on the other. He let her handle her own reins but ran a length of lariat from his saddle horn to hers. "Just in case you get any stupid ideas. I don't feel like chasing after you again," he remarked. She remained silent as they rode and he caught the sideways glances she tossed at him. Finally, she turned one into words.

"What if I made you a promise?" she probed.

His glance was hard. "What kind of a promise?"

"You let me go my way and I'll come back and tell Conley the truth," she said. "Or I'll write it to him."

His frown almost held amusement. "You must think I've been eating loco weed."

Her face flushed. "I keep my word," she protested.

"Sure you do. You're real honest about everything," he snapped.

Her lips tightened and she looked away and he saw her cheeks color. His frown stayed as he watched her flush. It was no act. His sarcasm had really stung her. She was a strange little package and he made a mental note of her reaction. Maybe there was more than one way to reach her. He rode on in silence, pushed up over a little steep incline when he came on a small clearing. He felt Crystal Kent pull her horse to a halt.

"I've got to stop," she said, bending over the saddle horn. "I'm feeling sick. Dizzy . . . my stomach hurts." He halted, swung from the saddle, and watched her slide from her horse, take a few tentative steps, then sink down to the ground, bend over with her hands to her stomach. "Nerves, I guess," she said. "And exhaustion. Had an attack yesterday." He watched her for a moment and she lifted her head. "Get me some water, please. In my canteen," she said, her voice tight.

He walked to the other side of her horse, found her canteen beside her saddlebag. He untied it, opened it, and moved to where she knelt, bent over. He squatted down beside her, started to reach out with the canteen. She began to pull herself up when suddenly her right hand came around in a sharp arc. As he flung himself sideways, he glimpsed the rock in it. The blow caught him alongside the temple, and though he'd managed to avoid the full force of it, he felt his eyes grow foggy, her shape become a shimmering, watery thing. He reached out for her, but she twisted away and he fell forward, shook his head, glimpsed the wavering form running. He cursed, shook his head again. The fog began to clear. She was just leaping onto the horse, and Fargo, pressing his hand down on the ground, and ignoring the ankle he'd injured yesterday, catapulted himself forward. He felt another wave of dizziness sweep over him, shook it away, dived as she came past, arms outstretched. He felt his hands catch onto wool, cloth, hang on as he was dragged, and then he felt her pulled sideways, off the saddle. He kept his hold as she came off altogether, fell with her, the swish of air passing over his head as the horse's rear hooves went over him. She landed half atop him; he rolled with her and she tried to twist away, managed to free herself from one hand.

82

He lashed out, felt the blow land against her leg, and heard her gasp of pain, rolled away again as she kicked. He grabbed her leg, yanked, and she came forward, gasping out curses, tried to twist away again. This time, his hand open, he caught her across the face. She cried out, flew in a half-somersault, to land on the ground on her rump. He was on his feet at once, standing over her, and he felt the trickle of blood from his temple. He reached down, one hand closing around her shirt, yanked her half up. She lifted one hand to her face, fear in her eyes now.

"Damn, you try that again and I'll knock your head off," he hissed at her.

She kept the hand to her face, but he saw the fear pushed aside by rage in her eyes. "You let me go, damn you," she flung back. He flung her backward and she hit the ground, the breath gasping out of her.

"When you start talking, damn your little hide," he said.

She gulped air, glared up at him. "Bastard," she said.

"Bitch," he returned. She rubbed one hand against her cheek and he saw the red welt across her cheekbone. The sticky trickle on his temple dispelled any remorse he might have had. He reached down, grabbed her shirt again, and yanked her to her feet. For an instant the fright flew into her eyes, but only for an instant. "Get on the damn horse," he growled. She did as he ordered and managed to be both beautiful and sullen at the same time. Damn hard to do, he conceded silently.

He let her ride a half-pace ahead of him as he wiped his temple dry and studied Crystal Kent with narrowed eyes. She sat her horse straight, the soft wind blowing her hair. One thing had become clear.

She hadn't fled the Kent ranch because she'd heard he'd broken jail. Not just for that. She hadn't been running from him as much as she had been to something. She was afraid of only one thing: being delayed, held back. She wanted to be someplace as quickly as possible, someplace very important to her. The truth he wanted out of her was tied to that, he was certain. The panic in her eyes at the thought of being held by him was still the best route to her, but perhaps he'd try riding it a different way. He pulled up alongside her.

"I don't like this any more'n you do," he said reasonably. "I don't want to keep you here, but I've got my own neck to think about." He caught the quick glance she tossed at him, kept his voice calm, relaxed. "All you have to do is tell the truth to Conley and you can be on your way," he said. She didn't turn, kept her eyes straight ahead, but he saw the tightening of her facial muscles. "Well, you think some more about it," he said easily. He rode alongside her, climbing up the narrow pathway that edged the base of the mountain. "What'd you tell them at that wagon train?" he asked casually.

"I told them I was being chased by a man who'd tried to kidnap me to make me marry him," she answered.

Fargo nodded. It was a story most people would buy, especially looking at the beauty of her. Crystal Kent could think quickly. He decided to try a shot to catch her off guard. "Why'd you marry Kent?" he asked casually. She flung an instant glance at him, pulled it away just as quickly. But he'd touched something again. It was all wrapped up together, inside that beautiful little package. All he had to do was get it out of her and be sure she'd stick to telling the truth. And stay out of Bloodhound Conley's hands until he'd done it. That could well be the hardest part. Conley would pick up the new trail without trouble, two horses now where there'd been only one. Fargo made a face, spurred the pinto on a little faster, felt the other horse follow as the lariat attached pulled on him. Fargo turned a little jog in the path and pulled back hard on the reins. The pinto dug heels into the ground and stopped abruptly; Fargo reached out, yanked Crystal Kent's horse back.

He put a finger to his lips, nodded down to a small gulley just below where they rode. She followed his gesture and he saw her eyes grow wide as she spied the line of Arapahos hidden just back of the trees. All but two were in the saddle and the two on foot were in the darker shadows of the trees, peering out beyond the tree line. Fargo followed their gaze, but he knew already what they were watching. The line of Conestogas plodded toward the bottom of the foothills, totally unaware of what lay in wait for them.

His eyes went back to the line of Arapaho below, copper bodies glistening in the sun, each one poised, leaning forward on his horse. Most carried bows, some held lances, but a few had carbines, he noted. Each of the two in the trees wore a single war feather at the back of his head. "Leaders," he murmured grimly. He felt Crystal Kent's eyes on him, looked at her.

"The wagon train," she whispered. "You've got to warn them."

He saw the Arapaho edge forward, start to spread out through the trees at a signal from one of the leaders. He pulled the pinto back, away from the edge of the path, taking the girl with him back around the little jog in the trail.

"We've got to warn the wagon train," she repeated.

"I'm not out here to play Good Samaritan," he said.

Her eyes, wide, turned darker, and she frowned at him. "What kind of man are you?" she hissed.

"One who's out here to save his neck, not lose it," he returned.

"You can't just let them walk into this. You've got to warn them, give them a chance," she said.

"Give you a chance to take off. That's what you really mean, isn't it?"

"No, dammit," she flung back. "I promise I won't take off."

He almost believed her. Almost. "You wouldn't think of it," he said.

"I'll go with you if you ride down and warn them," she said. "Dammit, didn't you see the kids in those wagons? You just going to let them be slaughtered without a chance?"

She swung down from the saddle and the anger in her eyes was real as she went to the edge of the little trail, peered down to where the Indians were still poised in wait. "They won't have a chance. They won't even get to form a stand," she murmured, turning back to him.

"Probably not," he agreed quietly.

"And you're just going to let it happen?" she accused.

"I'm not going to just let it happen. I can't stop it," he said.

"You mean, you won't."

"I mean that I followed you all this damn way because you're my ticket to avoid being hung and I'm not throwing that away for anybody or anything. The people in that wagon train know what they face coming out here, or they damn well ought to know. They'll have to handle it on their own."

"You could fire a shot and at least warn them."

"No shot," Fargo said.

"You really are a bastard," she threw back.

"Maybe, but I'm going to be a live bastard," he told her.

"I'll scream. They'll hear me. It'll carry," she said, opened her mouth. He clapped his hand over her face, pressed her backward to the ground. She tried to bite, get her mouth open to scream, and he slapped her hard.

"Stop it, you little fool," he hissed at her, keeping one hand over her mouth, staring into the rage of her eyes. "Those aren't the only redskins waiting. There's another band somewhere near. I know how the Arapaho fight. They won't commit themselves all at once. If you scream, they'll be on top of us." Her eyes, still seething, searched his, unsure of whether to believe him. "Dammit, we can't help them, not without committing suicide. They'll have to fight for themselves. Shots and screams won't help them. There's no time, no way, do you hear me?"

He saw the pain, real pain and anguish, come into her eyes, and suddenly, as if to seal his words, the air split apart with high-pitched cries and the explosion of horses breaking into a gallop. The attack had begun. Fargo pulled her up into a sitting position, took his hand from her mouth. Her eyes were wide as the wild shouts of the Arapaho hung in the air. Fargo motioned with his hand for her to keep silent and pulled her to her feet. The shouts from below were punctuated by rifle fire now. He motioned for her to follow as he walked the pinto up the steep slope through the trees, leading the way until he reached a small shelflike protuberance on the side of the slope. The scene below became visible from the shelf and he halted. The wagons had managed to form a double line as the Arapaho made darting sweeps at them. One Conestoga was already starting to burn from a fire arrow.

The cries, shouts, and gunfire were as clear as the sight of it and the cries of the Arapaho and the screams of the settlers when arrows struck home all mingled together in a terrible chorus. He saw the horror in Crystal Kent's face and his hand nudged her elbow. She glanced at him, saw him nod to an opening in the trees below at the far right. The second band of Arapaho were filing through, and as Fargo and the girl looked on, the warriors burst into the open to fling themselves into the attack. They circled counterclockwise to the first group and Fargo saw another of the Conestogas burst into fire.

He felt the girl's hand dig into his arm as a woman emerged from the burning wagon, two youngsters, a boy and a girl, close behind her. A dozen arrows hit them almost as one, turning the three forms into human pincushions, and he heard Crystal Kent scream, turn her head into his chest. "Oh, God, oh, my God," she said, gasping, digging her hands into him. He looked over the flame hair, watched the attack as the Arapaho broke through one set of the wagons, circled, came in from the other side. Three more of the Conestogas were afire as he turned away, led the girl to the horses.

"Saddle up," he said, half-boosted her onto the horse. Swinging up on the pinto, he set off through the trees of the slope, letting the pinto pick his pace. The screams followed for too long and he saw Crystal Kent put her hands to her ears. She rode that way until finally he halted. "You can let go now," he said, pulling one arm down from her head.

"I can still hear them," she half-whispered.

"In your head," he said. He rode on, leading her along, crossed a ridge, and circled back part of the way along a small path that led nowhere. He struck out through the trees again, found a mountain stream, slid down from the saddle. The woods were growing darker. "We'll make camp here," he said.

She dismounted, and as the day drew to an end, the air grew cool. He got a small fire started. "I've a can of beans in my saddlebag," she offered.

"Good," he said. "Get them." He watched her go to the horse, rummage in the saddlebag, and return with the beans. "Got anything more in there?" he asked.

"Enough for three or four days, I guess," she said. He made a mental note at once. She'd figured to be riding at least half that long, allowing time for extra rations. He made a quick estimate, saw that would have put her on the other side of the mountains, just below South Pass and just before the giant Tetons rose up. He filed the information in his head, finished cooking the beans, and they ate in silence as the night closed around them. In the firelight, her hair seemed part of the flame, little glints of fire catching in it.

"I wonder what happened," she murmured solemnly. "Did some of them hold out?"

He said nothing and she pried with her glance. "They could have made it, some of them, at least," she said. Once again he stayed silent. "You always look at the worst side of things?" she demanded angrily.

"No, just the real side. There's no percentage in anything else," he answered.

"It must be terrible to live that way," she snapped. "What way?"

"Never having any hope, any faith in anyone or anything," she said.

"I'm full of hope all the time," he answered. "I just don't let hoping get in the way of seeing."

She lapsed into silence again and stared at the fire,

and somehow she managed to make her silence accusing. He drank in the beauty of her as the firelight set her hair aglow and her breasts rose under the dark-green shirt to let little deep half-moon shadows cup them from underneath. She seemed made of contradictions, he pondered. She'd put his neck in a noose without batting an eyelash, yet she'd been willing to risk her life to warn the wagon train. She'd told a bald-faced dirty lie about him to Conley, yet she was genuinely hurt when he hadn't believed that she'd keep her word about coming back to tell the truth. It didn't add up. In fact, damn little added up about Crystal Kent.

"I'm going to turn in," she said, breaking into his thoughts as she got to her feet.

"Put your bedroll by that tree there." He pointed.

"Why?" she asked.

"You'll be uncomfortable anyplace else," he said blandly, saw suspicion start to slide across her face.

"What's that mean?" she pressed.

"It means that by that tree you'll have enough slack in the rope to turn over if you want," he said mildly, and watched suspicion turn into a frown.

"Rope to turn over? You mean you're going to tie me up?" she questioned.

"Go to the head of the class," he said, getting up.

"You really are rotten," she spit out.

"I'm damn tired and I intend to get some sleep. I can't do it keeping one eye on you," he said.

She eyed him for a moment. "I suppose you wouldn't believe me if I promised not to run away," she offered.

"You suppose right, honey," he said.

Her lovely face grew set again. "I can't sleep tied up," she said.

"Crap. You'll sleep," he told her.

She glared at him for a moment. "Is it all right if I

get my things and change?" she asked, ice in each word.

"Go ahead. Pick a tree and change behind it," he said evenly as he kicked ashes onto the fire. He watched her as she went to her horse, took down her bedroll, and rummaged through her saddlebag. He saw her bring out a long-handled hairbrush, a handful of hairpins, some ribbons. He concentrated on putting out the fire and, out of the corner of his eyes, saw her step behind a tree. He got his own bedroll, heard her being busy behind the tree, and when she emerged, she had her green shirt and jodhpurs in hand, her nightdress on, and her hair atop her head. She still looked damn beautiful. She carried her things to the tree he'd pointed out to her, put her bedroll nearby it, and turned to him.

"What next?" she tossed at him.

He took the lariat from the pinto and stepped to her. She kept her eyes on his, deep pinpoints of rage, as he tied her ankles together first, lowered her to the ground. Then he took the lariat and bound her wrists in front of her, crossing one over the other, leaving her free to move her fingers. He ran the wrist rope around the tree trunk, tightened it, looked over at her.

"Lay down and turn over on your bedroll," he said and she obeyed. He allowed a little more slack in the rope, then knotted it back of the tree. If she tried hobbling her way to it, he'd certainly hear her. She had use of her fingers to pull on her blanket, enough slack to turn over, but not enough to reach her ankles.

He pulled her blanket over her. "You'll sleep just fine," he told her.

She glared up at him. "You going to do this every night?" she asked.

"Depends. Some nights I might just hold on to

91

you myself," he said evenly, saw her eyes narrow. He turned from her, felt her eyes as he took off his shirt and chaps, then his trousers, slid under the bedroll across the now-dead fire from her. He turned his back to her, felt the weariness of his body in a sudden rush. He was asleep in moments, his body demanding its price for the last stretch of tense, hard-riding days and nights. The cool mountain air blew over him, soothing, lulling, nature's wine.

5

When the dawn filtered down through the trees, Fargo woke, blinked sleep from his eyes. He turned over, squinted across the ashes at Crystal Kent's bedroll. He blinked again, his eyes opening wide. "Shit!" The single word exploded from his lips as he bounded from the bedroll. She was gone, her bedroll lying empty. He took a moment to really believe his eyes. There was no way she could have gotten the rope untied and no way she could have reached the tree to untie it without waking him. Yet she was sure as hell gone, the rope on the ground. He was at the empty bedroll in one long stride, kneeling down, examining the lariat.

"Goddamn," he muttered. She hadn't untied it at all. He held up one length of the rope. It had been cut, cleanly severed. He stared down at it and knew it could have been done only one way—with a knife. Or a razor, perhaps. He'd left no knots to undo at her wrists and she couldn't reach below her waist. Yet she'd hidden a knife. Only one place, between her luscious breasts. "Damn," he murmured again. When she'd fixed her hair and put the nightdress on, she'd put a knife between her breasts, maybe held it there with one of her hair ribbons. The rope allowed her enough slack to reach it after he was hard asleep and she could hold it in her fingers and slowly saw away at the wrist ropes. He could see her doing it, using the knife in short motions. It'd no doubt taken her damn near the whole night to cut her wrists free. But once that was done, she could reach down and untie her ankles. She'd lain the severed lariat carefully on the ground, leaving the other end still tied around the tree.

Glancing up, he saw something else. She'd taken her saddlebag and bedroll but left her horse. Smart, he grunted in grudging appreciation. Taking the horse would undoubtedly have wakened him. He uttered another oath, spun around, and dived into his clothes. He threw his bedroll together and vaulted onto the pinto, took her horse by the reins and set off after her. She hadn't much of a start and on foot she'd not make much time. He picked up her tracks easily enough in the dew-wet grass and leaves, followed, frowning, the frown growing deeper with every passing moment. She had headed down to where the wagon train had been attacked.

"Goddamn," he swore aloud again, spurring the pinto forward into a trot. Alarm and fear held his face as he swept the ground with his eyes. The trail kept going downward. He'd been right. She'd struck out for the wagon train. She was hopeful there'd been survivors and she figured to hitch up with them or go back to the wide pass where she'd first been heading. "Stupid little package," he murmured, and damned the curse of the inexperienced.

She could well find more than survivors. It was a six-wagon train with two supply wagons. The Arapaho wouldn't just race off when finished. They had plenty of time and lots of things to pick over. They'd have themselves a good time with whatever survivors were left. He had seen Indians take twenty-four hours picking over their booty.

His eyes saw her trail suddenly go down a steep incline, saw where she'd clung to branches to lower herself. Too steep for the horse, he hurried on, raced along the path that finally doubled back to the bottom of the steep incline. He saw where she'd landed, gone on, and then, almost abruptly, the remains of the wagon train lay ahead of him. His eyes swept the charred skeletons of the wagons, limp figures hung over their sides like so many twisted rag dolls. He saw a handful of buzzards already on the ground and he hurried the pinto to the scene, the buzzards flying up at once, their giant gray wings and bald heads lifting over his form to join the others still slowly making wide circles in the sky. His eyes disregarded the anguish and horror in front of him. It was past, done with. No pity on his part could change any of it, no revulsion help anything now.

The Trailsman's eyes swept the ground. Too many marks to pick out her footprints. If, indeed, they were here. But beyond the area of the attack he found a new trail of unshod hooves, the Arapaho moving on. He dismounted, examined them. Not more than a few hours old, perhaps not more than two. Some of the horses were heavily laden, carrying two riders or loot they were bringing back. He swung onto the pinto and hurried after the trail. It led along the edge of the foothills and he galloped to close distance, then slowed to a canter as the trail turned and moved into the low hills.

Maybe they didn't have her, he pondered. Maybe

she hadn't walked in on them. Maybe she'd seen them in time and had been able to vanish into the woods. And then maybe they'd seen her first. Dammit, he had to know. He had to find out. He'd no choice but to find out if his one chance to clear himself was to be lost on the wall of an Arapaho tepee. He had to know and, by God, do something about it if he could. *If he could.* The words repeated themselves inside him, an ominous litany. He spurred the pinto on again, kept riding hard until suddenly he glimpsed the tiny figures in the distance, moving easily, slowly into the foothills. He turned the horse, rode upward into the hills, and leveled out, moved forward ahead of the Arapaho. He turned again, found a spot looking down from a collection of sandstone boulders. He was dismounted and waiting as the Arapaho came into close view just slightly below.

His lips moved in a soundless oath as he spotted her at once, on a horse between two lance-carrying bucks, her hair standing out like firethorn on a snowbank. They had her hands tied behind her and he saw the fear in the deep-brown eyes. Yet she still looked beautiful. Some of the Arapaho rode two on a pony as they passed below, some trailing clothes and cotton goods from their ponies. "Goddamn you, Crystal Kent," he whispered. "I'd like to race down there and kick your little ass in, myself."

Fargo watched the procession move on, the last of the Indian ponies going on ahead. He waited, then swung onto the pinto again and followed, keeping well out of sight. There was damn little chance for Crystal Kent and even less to get her free. But he had to try. He had to see if he could find some way. He turned ideas in his mind as he stayed back of the Indians. One thing could help him. They wouldn't skewer her through right away, not with that hair and that body. She'd be worth keeping alive for a

95

while. It would give him perhaps a half-dozen extra hours. Could he do a damn thing with them? The question mocked as he dogged the Arapaho.

Suddenly he reined up, his eyes catching the three poles of the Arapaho tepee jutting into the air. He turned the pinto, moved on through a stand of thick oak trees to move within sight of the full camp. He slid from the saddle, tied the horses, and crept forward on foot until he was but a half-dozen yards from the camp. The girl had been taken from the horse, hands still bound behind her back. A cluster of young bucks gazed at her, touching the flame-red hair. Fargo watched as the squaws came to gather around her, mostly old ones but with a few young mixed in. They cackled like hens, and one old toothless crone poked a stick at her while another pointed to her boots. One of the braves pushed the old squaw away. Fargo watched Crystal Kent's face and had to admire the way she kept her jaw tight and refused to let fear show in her face.

One of the young bucks stepped closer to her, reached out with both hands, and pulled the green shirt from her, ripping if off so that only one sleeve stayed dangling. In seconds, the squaws moved in and did the rest, stripping her naked, pulling boots from her, tearing off petticoat and bloomers. Fargo heard Crystal's scream from inside the cluster of squaws, more terror than pain as a tall buck chased the women away, then stepped back himself. Fargo took in the girl's naked beauty, even now, in this setting, a breathtaking beauty, breasts full and rounded yet high, small pink nipples, flat with tiny pink areolae, virginal in appearance. Her stomach, slightly convex, thoroughly sensuous, legs beautifully long yet full, a ripe, throbbing figure. Fargo saw the squaws giggle and point to the black triangle against the cream-alabaster skin, so thick, bushy, and full compared to those of most Indian women. As they chattered and giggled, one reached out, drew her hand across the soft-wire thickness of it, and let out a high-pitched half-laugh, half-cry. Crystal shrank back and one of the bucks barked at the squaw, who instantly stepped back.

Fargo watched the Indian move to Crystal, run his hand through the flame hair, and saw two more bucks step forward to do the same thing. Then abruptly, almost yanking her from her feet, they pulled her sideways to a pole staked in the ground. With a half-dozen deft coils, she was bound to it and they left her there, striding away. The squaws broke into small groups and drifted away also. Crystal Kent was being left for bigger and better things yet to come.

The Trailsman settled down to watch and wait. There was little else to do now. He let his eyes roam over the camp while his mind tried to form some kind of plan. The camp was large, a longhouse and a meat-drying frame at the far end. In the Arapaho fashion, they used the narrow-based tepee, arranged in a three-quarter double circle. The line of tepees came close to the oaks where he lay hidden at the right end of the circle. They were used by the older squaws and the young, yet-unspoken-for girls, he saw. So far, only one thing had gone as he'd hoped. They were keeping Crystal Kent alive, to pleasure themselves with her, in their ways. When they finished, she'd no longer be beautiful, of course. But especially brave foes and especially beautiful ones always got special treatment. It was an unhappy honor for those on the receiving end.

Again, his eyes roamed across the camp. If there was a chance, it would be a damn slim one. And it would have to be quick and brutal, no time for anything but total savagery. If there was a chance, he murmured again. He shifted his position, settled down to wait. A handful of Indian kids came up to stare at the girl; one touched her tentatively, then ran off with the others. Fargo saw the fear in her eyes, yet the tightness of her jaw, as she refused to give in to terror. She was made of many things, he decided, a kind of stupid, stubborn courage being one of them.

Maybe she deserved what she faced, he reflected. Maybe she'd lied other men into other nooses. But he didn't give a tinker's damn about poetic justice. He needed her alive, able to tell the truth. He pressed back deeper into the trees, rested his head on his arm, and let the hours pass, half-asleep, the sounds of the camp a quiet hum as the dark descended. He stretched his muscles without changing position, lifted his head up to survey the camp. Her magnificent naked form still held all its beauty, the brilliant tresses falling partly over the stake at her back. His glance moved to the center of the camp, where a large fire was lighted, and he saw the squaws bringing meat to cook, corncakes to heat. The fire sent its light almost to the edges of the camp, and Fargo watched the Indians gather to eat, their voices a low drone.

He eyed Crystal Kent, glanced at her saddlebag, considered trying to make it to her, cut her free, and run. A half-dozen kids ran by and he discarded the thought at once. Not enough time and too many unexpected possibilities in the way. He settled down, crept forward to the edge of the trees, and waited until the meal was finished. Four braves detached themselves from the others and walked to where Crystal was tied. A dozen or more older squaws followed them. The old toothless one hobbled in the forefront. The braves examined Crystal Kent, then stepped back, barked at the squaws. Instantly, the women were at the girl, pushing and poking, grabbing at her, digging nails into her legs. In seconds, they had untied her, the old toothless one leading all the others in throwing the girl to the ground. A single-strand rawhide whip appeared in her hand, and she struck at the girl and Fargo heard Crystal's scream. The old crone kept flailing with the single thong of rawhide, and Fargo saw Crystal Kent rolling on the ground, trying to avoid the blows. Others kicked at her and leaned forward to hit her with their hands. Crystal was gasping out half-sobs and curses. One stumpy squaw grabbed her long hair and pulled, and Crystal's scream rose, to be cut off in a sharp gasp as a moccasined foot caught her in the stomach.

One of the braves barked again at the squaws—a hard, stern command—and then walked off with the others. Fargo saw the women grab Crystal, start to drag her into the tepee to his right. His lips formed the silent words as he watched helplessly. It was only a beginning. The squaws had been told they could have their fun with her first, aware they were but a preliminary to the coming day. That was the custom, the way such things were always done. Crystal Kent disappeared inside the tepee, dragged in by the hair, screaming, and from inside the tent he heard the slapping sounds and more gasped cries of pain from the girl. Her voice died away for a few moments, only the sound of the squaws' cackling heard. Fargo pushed himself forward, scanned the rest of the camp. It was pretty much settled down for the night, the fire burning down in the distant center of the camp.

Crystal Kent screamed again and he could hear her words, high-pitched, on the edge of panic. "No, oh, God, please no . . . no . . . oh, no!" A scream ended the words, and Fargo pushed forward on his stomach, inching closer to the tepee as he let his glance ring the camp once more. The Arapaho had posted no sentries. They felt secure here. "Oh, God, no . . . Jesus . . . ooooh, no!" Crystal's voice cut through the night again, hysteria in it. The cackling of the old squaws mingled with her pleading screams.

He reached the tepee, drew the razor-sharp throwing knife from his leg holster, paused, sniffed the air. He smelled something burning, sharp, slightly acrid. The girl screamed again, and Fargo raised the knife, rested it against the tepee. He pushed with the very tip, exerting a slow steady pressure until he felt the hide give way. Carefully, he pulled the edge of the blade down along the hide of the tepee to make a short, vertical slit, just enough for him to press one eye against. Crystal shrieked again, real terror, and he peered in, found her naked form on the floor, two squaws holding her arms stretched over her head, two her legs. The old toothless crone stood over her with a stick, glowing hot at one end from the small fire to one side of the tepee. As Fargo watched, she pressed the stick against the thick, bushy black triangle, and Crystal shrieked again. Fargo saw the wisp of smoke rise from her pubic hair and knew the odor he'd smelled, that of burned hair and singed flesh.

He saw the squaws pull Crystal Kent's legs apart and up, opening her fully to the old squaw. The toothless one heated the end of the stick, knelt down, cackling, and poked the red-hot end forward between the outspread legs of Crystal Kent. She moved it closer and Crystal's scream of pure terror almost shook the tepee. Cackling, the old crone pushed the burning end of the stick still closer, hardly an inch away from the waiting opening. Crystal's scream became an agonized shriek and snapped off abruptly as she passed out.

A chorus of laughter rose from the squaws as the old crone pulled the stick back. She wouldn't have plunged the red-hot end into the girl, Fargo knew. The old crone knew it, too. The braves would have skinned her alive for that. But Crystal Kent hadn't known it, and so the squaws had enjoyed the refinements of terror, pain often more real than physical pain itself. He drew a deep breath, took his eye from the slit for a moment, and scanned the camp. It was still quiet and he returned to the slit.

They were tossing water onto Crystal and he saw the girl come about, half-sit up, the terror still hard in her eyes. The stumpy squaw dealt her a blow across the face that knocked her onto her back again. It seemed a signal and suddenly the single rawhide thong whips were in everyone's hands. They flipped the girl onto her stomach and lashed at her with the leather thongs. They confined themselves to the back of her legs.and her buttocks, both soon crimson red with streaks of welts. Finally they stopped, and Crystal, sobbing, gasping, lay with her legs drawn up to her stomach. A few stray blows had left marks across her back and shoulders.

Fargo's eyes were blue agate and he unclenched his fists to bring circulation back into his fingers. "Damn the girl," he murmured. She'd brought it all on herself by her fool escaping, but his pity for her was not for now. She'd experienced nothing compared to what lay in store for her when the braves took over. His eye against the slit in the hide saw most of the squaws preparing to leave the tepee. They'd had their fun. More was forbidden them. Three of the women pulled Crystal onto her back and tied her by the wrists to stakes driven into the ground. He watched as a young girl came to squat down beside her, run her hands over the flame hair, then down across the full breasts, doing so with the exploratory curiosity of a child. He glanced again at the young girl. She wasn't much more than a child. The girl got to her feet and followed the other squaws as they started to leave the tepee.

Fargo scooted backward from the tepee, backing himself into the line of trees like a raccoon backing into a hole. He watched most of the squaws file from the tepee and hurry to their own tents. As he lay still, waiting for them to quiet down, he saw two braves moving silently around the edge of the camp, circling the tepee carefully. They were obviously a patrol. There had to be others, Fargo knew, the camp too large for a patrol of just two. He watched, flattened to the ground, as the braves moved on, disappeared into the darkness of the rest of the camp. He lay silently, waiting, until the camp was quiet once again. He began to inch his way forward once more, this time making a slow circle around the tepee, staying on his stomach, until he neared the closed entrance flap. He waited, listened, let his eyes move across the ground, scanning the other tepees. The two braves could return this way at any moment. Things could fall in on him at any second.

Fargo put his ear to the flap. Rasping breathing drifted to him, and a quiet soft sobbing. He drew the throwing knife out again, though there'd be no throwing now. It would have to be close quarters and brutal, and he felt his lips draw back in distaste. He didn't relish the thought of what he had to do. Yet there was no other way, no time for anything less savagely final. He couldn't allow one scream, not one gasped cry. His only chance was speed and silence. His and Crystal Kent's only chance, he corrected himself. Carefully, he pushed up the tent flap, just enough to let himself slide in on his stomach. He

102

paused, let his eyes grow used to the shadowed dimness inside the tepee. The small fire surrounded by stones still burned to one side, affording enough flickering light for him to see.

The old crone lay asleep on a pallet along the far side of the tepee. Another elderly squaw slept curled up on the ground along the other half of the circle. Midway between them, a young girl lay asleep on a blanket, her deerskin dress folded beside her. She looked more like a boy than a young girl, thin, supple body with hardly any breasts, eyes closed in a face of sharp planes. Only Crystal Kent was awake, he saw, eyes staring up at the top of the tepee. He lifted himself into a crouch, moved with the quickness of a puma, saw Crystal turn her head, catch sight of him. He was at her in an instant, clapping one hand over her mouth. Her eyes looked at him over the edge of his hand, came alive with sudden hope. He cut her wrist bonds with two slashes of the blade but pushed her back as she tried to sit up. He pressed her down to the ground, spoke to her with his eyes, and she nodded understanding, let herself relax.

He turned from her and the wave of revulsion swept over him again. But it had to be done. The squaws would scream the entire camp into action if they came awake, and he reminded himself of one truth: were positions reversed, they wouldn't think twice about doing the same to him. One stride put him alongside the toothless old crone. "You've had many summers, old woman," he murmured, "and tortured many victims. Your time has come." She started to turn, come awake, and he swept the knife blade across her throat in one quick arc, turning from her even before the gush of red bubbled from her. At the second old squaw, the deed was done again in a silent split second. He went to the young girl, looked down at her, the red-stained blade in his hand. Skye Fargo's jaw muscles throbbed, and suddenly he reached down, yanked the girl up by one arm. As she snapped awake, his fist hit the point of her jaw and she fell back onto the blanket, unconscious. He spun around and motioned, and Crystal sat up, started to pull herself to her feet, her face twisting in pain. She reached out, grasped hold of the girl's wide, loose deerskin dress, slipped it over her shoulder, and stood up.

Fargo, at the tent flap, peered out at the bottom as he lifted the hide, motioned to Crystal not to move. The two braves were making another round and he watched them go past, eyes searching the dark borderline of the camp. He waited till they'd disappeared from sight, then dropped to his stomach, motioned for Crystal to follow. She came down beside him and he pushed forward under the tent flap, sheathing the knife as he did so. She crawled beside him as he slowly made his way around the tepee, moving over a few yards to retrieve the saddlebag that still lay on the ground. He reached the dark oaks, the girl alongside him. He got to his feet, pulled her up with him to look sharply at her. She was at the thin edge of collapse, panic in her eyes, and he felt the trembling of her body.

"Hold on a little longer," he said softly. "Step carefully. Watch with your toes. Stay off twigs." He led her forward until the dark shape of the horses came into sight. "Can you ride?" he asked. "On your own?"

"Yes," she whispered, her voice hoarse. "I think so." He helped her mount up, saw her wince, hold herself still in pain as her legs settled down over the horse, the raw skin of the whipped areas pulling open. He watched her, frowning, and she drew a deep breath, nodded at him. "I'll be all right," she said. He took the pinto and led the way, breaking into a canter only when he was certain they were far enough away not to be heard. He knew Crystal Kent hurt with every movement of the horse, but he kept riding, turning one way then another, staying in areas almost impossible to follow. The dawn rose and he found a narrow passageway into a small mountain glade. They'd come back a good distance from the camp. The Arapaho would send out search parties, but not this far. They'd not make a big thing of a woman escaping from their clutches.

He turned into the passage and halted in the tree-covered safety of the glade, dismounted, and saw Crystal still sitting in the saddle, holding on to the horn, her face drawn. He reached up, took her down as she gasped out in pain, set her gently on the grass. She sank down to the ground at once, bending almost double, her hands held to her stomach. He knelt down beside her. "What hurts most?" he asked.

She half-turned, shuddered, licked her lips, slowly moved her hand, touched the singed pubic area with one finger. He rose, went to his own saddlebag, found the small vial after a moment, and returned to her. He started to lift the deerskin dress. Her hand grabbed his wrists, protest in her eyes, an automatic reaction. He halted, looked at her. "Want to stop hurting?" he asked quietly, holding the vial higher. "Balm of Gilead buds, comfrey, and cocoa-butter salve. Best damn thing for burns and cuts."

She wrestled with herself and he took her hand from his wrist, pushed the Indian dress up again gently. "Come on now. I've seen it all anyway," he said.

She turned her head, looked away as he pushed the deerskin up to her rounded little belly. He uncorked the vial and began to rub the salve into the singed hair and the parts of her skin that had been scalded. She whimpered some, but the salve soothed almost at once as he carefully applied it to the soft-wire nap, rubbing it in with slow gentle strokes.

"Never rubbed one of these for this reason," he remarked idly as his fingers traveled along the small soft mound beneath the bush covering.

She continued to keep her head turned to the side and he applied more of the salve to the back of her legs and delicious little rear. He rose then, pulled the Indian dress down, and put the vial back into his saddlebag. He stretched out beside her as the morning sun covered them with a warm blanket. "Get some sleep," he told her, and felt the ache in his own body. She half-turned against him, buried her face into his chest. The night had been made of terror, savagery, and exhaustion. It was time for sleep and nothing more, but he knew he'd remember, when he woke, how good the soft alabaster body felt against his, how sweet the velvet skin under his fingers.

6

He woke when he felt her stir. She'd slept restlessly at first, waking often to half-scream, trembling violently, then settling down against him each time. Finally she'd slept without waking until now. He watched through eyelids barely opened as she rose, stretched, managed to look beautiful despite everything that had happened. She rose, went to her saddlebag, and pulled out a blue shirt and a loose gray skirt. He stirred, sat up on one elbow, and she half-spun, sudden alarm in her eyes.

"Easy," he said, saw her draw in a deep breath.

"My nerves are raw," she said. "I hear a brook just past those trees. I'm going to wash." She plucked at the Indian dress on her. "And get this thing off," she said, shuddering.

He nodded and she disappeared back of the black oaks. He heard the sounds of her at the brook as he got to his feet, went to the horses, and examined each one. They were both in good enough shape, feet solid and free of sores. When Crystal returned, she had the blue shirt and the skirt on, her hair shimmering in the sun.

"Half the day is gone, isn't it?" she said.

"More than half," he said. "But you needed the sleep. We both did."

She shuddered. "I won't ever forget, ever," she said.

"You only got a taste," he told her.

"It was horrible . . . all of it," she said, and he knew what she meant. Her eyes studied him, her head leaning to one side. "You're one of a kind, aren't you?" she remarked.

"I do what has to be done," he said.

She stepped to him. "And I'm alive because of that. I won't forget," she told him.

"Tell Conley the truth about what happened at the Kent ranch. That'll make us even," he said.

Her face set itself at once, but he saw the stab of pain in the deep eyes. "No," she said. "I'm sorry. Really, I am."

He studied her eyes. No acting. Once again, she was wrestling with something deep and powerful inside her.

"You'll talk," he said flatly, the edge of a threat on the words.

She stepped to him, looked up with her eyes round and full of honesty. "Look, the sooner you let me go my way, the faster I can come back and tell what really happened," she said.

"The sooner you tell the truth, the sooner you can be on your way," he countered.

"Trust me," she said. "I know that's asking a lot."

"Too damn much," he told her.

"Please," she begged.

"Can't, even if I'd a notion to. Suppose something happened to you. That'd leave me still facing a noose," he answered. He turned away brusquely, left the disappointment and dismay hanging in her eyes. "Mount up," he ordered. She followed him from the glade, came up alongside him.

"You are a hard man, Fargo," she commented.

"And you're stubborn," he answered. "Why the hell did you go back to the wagon train? That was especially stupid. I told you they wouldn't make it."

"I thought I could find a horse left there," she answered.

He grunted and rode on in silence, reaching the path that looked down to the passage the wagon train had been heading for. He reined up suddenly. The knot of horsemen appeared below, just starting to move through the mouth of the pass. They rode with steady purposefulness, and in the forefront Bloodhound Conley sitting his horse with ramrod straightness. Fargo's eyes took in the two outriders, each some twenty yards out on both sides of the main posse.

"Damn," he muttered, started to wheel the pinto. Crystal Kent was still staring down at the horsemen. "Move, dammit," he barked, yanking at her reins. She came up alongside him. He turned to go forward, caught her movement out of the corner of his eye, her arm flashing out toward him. He felt her hand close around the gun butt in his holster. He snapped his arm down as she yanked at the Remington, managed to pull it free. She started to lift it into the air, but he got a finger in front of the trigger before she could press off a shot. Reaching around with his other hand, he tore the gun from her grip; then, leaning sideways, he yanked her from her horse, pulling her onto his, facedown, lying across the saddle in front of him. He sent the pinto galloping forward, the other horse following.

"Oh, Jesus. The horn's breaking my ribs," he heard her cry.

"Tough shit," he snapped, but pushed back in the saddle to give her another inch of room. He heard her harsh gasps of breath as she bounced on her stomach with each thud of the horse's hooves. He climbed into the mountains, finally leveled off, and came to a halt. She slid from the saddle, to sink to the ground, holding both hands to her stomach, her breath still a long, harsh wheezing. He dropped to the ground, stood over her, reached down, and yanked her to her feet; his blue eyes were agate hard. "What the hell is with you?" he barked. "I save your damn scalp and you try to put my neck right back in a noose. You've a damn poor way of showing your gratitude."

"I'm sorry," she said. "Really, I am."

He glared at her. Her eyes were full of honesty and he found himself shaking his head at her. "What's going on with you?" he asked again.

The fear and the pain came into her eyes again. "It's me, that's all," she said. "I can't tell you."

"You mean you won't," he shot back roughly.

Her hands moved helplessly. "I can't."

Fear in her helplessness again, he saw, and the

wild panic coming into her eyes. "It wouldn't make you let me go," she said.

"It might. Try me," he said.

She shook her head, flame hair cascading from side to side. "I know better. It'd be just more words to you. You don't believe I'd come back. It wouldn't change that."

"Maybe it would," he tried, offering hope.

Her mouth tightened. "I can't take the chance. I don't know what you'd do. You're a hard man," she said.

"That's right," he said. "Mount up. We're moving on." He barked roughly at her, watched as she pulled herself into the saddle. "You'll talk sooner or later," he said. "You're just prolonging it and making it harder on yourself."

He saw her cast a glance back down the mountainside, turn her eyes on him for a moment, thin veils over them not disguising the hint of stubborn hope. "You think Conley will catch up," he said. "Forget it. I'll leave a trail that'll keep him running all over these mountains until it's winter and he has to quit." She didn't change expression as he peered at her with his eyes blue ice. "You see, honey, I've got all the time in the world."

Her lips turned in as she tore her eyes from his, slapped her horse on the rump, and took off in a fast canter. He caught up to her, swung alongside her as she slowed down. His words hadn't been entirely a lie. He could run Conley for a good while. But they hadn't been the truth either. Sooner or later, Conley would crawl up his tail. The pursuer always had the advantage. Conley had only to pursue, inch his way closer and closer while he had to pick and choose flight, find places to run and to hide, drag along Crystal and wrestle with her delaying tactics. Just looking over your shoulder put one at a disadvantage. The pursuer only looked forward. Conley was too damn close. He'd never be held away till winter.

Fargo glanced at Crystal. He had to get her to crack before Conley reached them. It was vital that she got no hopes up for a rescue. He led her along a winding, twisting pattern and saw her dismay, the set of her lovely face. It was having the effect he wanted on her. It wouldn't bother Conley all that much, he knew, but he was working on Crystal now. Finally he found a small spot as the night began to lower, a little rock-rimmed area with ample firewood and protected from wind and eye.

He got a small fire started and Crystal brought drief beef and a can of soup from her saddlebag, set about to cook. He let her, stretched out. The night stayed warm and the fire made the little area warmer. They ate in silence and she cleaned up when they finished. He took off his shirt and let the fire warm his body. Crystal Kent lay down near him, on one elbow, let her eyes travel over his hard-muscled, steel-spring frame, his smoothly tanned skin that fitted tight as a glove. He saw her eyes halt on the half-moon curve of the scar.

"How'd you get that?" she asked.

"Bear claw," he said. He reached for a piece of wood for the fire and she moved at the same moment. His hand touched hers, stayed there. She let the deep, liquid eyes hold his glance.

"I'm sorry it's not different," she said.

"Different?" he frowned.

"For us, the way we are. I'm sorry it's that way," she said.

"You can change that," he told her, saw her face stiffen at once. "Why'd you marry Howard Kent?" he asked, but she caught the snare in the question and

111

didn't answer. "Was he worth it in bed?" Fargo prodded.

Her lips pressed together. "He was an old man with a lot of worries. He never got it together during the month we were married."

"That disappoint you?" he probed.

"No," she said quickly.

He searched her face with his eyes. "You always waste that beauty of yours?" he asked. "That's a damn sin, you know."

Her eyes stayed on his. "Yes, I suppose it is. Sometimes it gets in the way. It makes you a target," she said. "I don't want to waste it."

He reached out, put a hand behind her slender, graceful neck. "I don't like waste. Not of beauty or of moments," he said.

"Are you asking?" she said.

"Not really. I could take," he told her.

"It'd be different."

"I know that. Especially with you," he said.

"Yes, you would understand that," she commented, her eyes studying him.

"Well?" he asked. "Is it yes?"

"Will it make a difference?" she asked. "For me? For what I want?"

"No bargaining. I want the real thing, not another act," he said.

"No act. I just want to know. Will it make a difference?" she asked, almost little-girl-like.

His eyes traveled down the firelit beauty of her. He'd know damn quick whether she was faking. "Sure it'll make a difference," he said.

She lifted her head, moved her lips to his, opened her mouth for him, honey-apple sweetness. She could kiss beautifully, her lips moist and soft and full. She let her tongue dart, just a flicker, then withdraw, and her lips parted still wider, invitation, surrogate opening. She drew in with her lips, pulling his tongue deep. His hands were unbuttoning the shirt, finding the full, round warmth of her magnificent breasts. He had seen them already, watched them as she writhed under beatings and bound to stakes, but it was different now. They throbbed for his touch and she pushed his face down between them. He felt her shudder as he closed his lips around the fullness of one, pulled on it, let the tiny, flat virginal tip begin to form into soft hardness.

"Oh, Fargo, Fargo, my God," she said, pushing herself up into his mouth. Her hands went around the back of his neck, pressing him down. The tiny tips were swollen now, begging for the soft touch of his mouth. He felt her shed the skirt, pull at his trousers, and in moments he was naked beside her. His hand went to the thick luxurious bush at her legs, and he remembered to be gentle.

"It's all right. It's all better," he heard her say, and let his hand caress the small pubic mound. "Yes, please yes," she coughed out, lifted her hips, sought his touch. He caressed the full velvet skin of her thighs slowly, running his hand down to the dark places, let his hand pause, hold, and she grew rigid. "No, don't stop. Oh, please, please," she half-screamed. He felt her hand clutching at him, almost wildly, and, his touch still holding at the very gates of the portal, he looked down at the utter beauty of hair, a halo of flame around the classic lines of her face, her lips parted, thirsting, wanting. She lifted again, cried out small whimpering pleas, and he let his hand move a fraction closer to the waiting portal. Again, she whimpered, thrust upward, and slowly he let his hand move against the wet, waiting lips, into the opening. "Ooooooh," she screamed softly, and her breath seemed to disappear as he slowly, slowly moved forward. She sank back, trembling, and her hands clutched at him.

"Come to me. Oh, please, come to me," she begged. No act. Most definitely no act, he noted as he moved atop her, let himself slide into the dark, warm haven. This time the scream was fuller, deeper, and as he moved with tantalizing slowness, her cries increased in rhythm. He brought her up to the edge of ecstasy, held her there as her fists beat a frantic little tattoo upon his back. Suddenly her matching thrustings grew frantic and he stayed with her, let her hang in midair as the cry circled the little rockbound area. "Oh, God, Fargo, oh, please hold me, hold me," she gasped into his shoulder.

He moved slowly inside her and she screamed, clung to him, fell back as he withdrew, and he heard the harsh sounds of her breathing. He lay beside her, drank in her beauty, watched as she turned on her side, one full breast lying over his chest. The deep, liquid eyes were black coals, and she moved her breasts against him, sliding down, their softness passing over his chest, across the hard-muscled abdomen, down farther until she held his maleness between the full pillowed softness. He rubbed back and forth with her breasts until his strength began to return, surging upward again. Her mouth made little moist trails across his belly, sought, and found; and he heard the gasp of pleasure from her. She stayed with him, caressing, pulling, enclosing, her own quiet reveling until he reached down, lifted her up, and swung over her once again. He pressed into the ripe, full magnificence of her, and this time she hurried less but cried out more. Her arms held him in a viselike grip and she cried out for more and more and time was lost in the warm, wet magic of her. When it happened this time, she held him in with her warm thighs and he could feel the spas-

114

modic contractions of her, gasps of the flesh, soundless words of approval.

He lay beside her later, the red hair spread over his chest, her face against his abdomen, her hand cradling him, warm between his legs. Finally, she pulled herself up on one elbow, her eyes finding his. "Satisfied?" she asked. "Think I was acting?"

"No," he conceded. "You wanted. I'm flattered."

"I've always been particular," she said. "It's too easy the other way." She sat up, reached for the shirt, and slipped it on. His hand halted her as she began to button. She let the shirt hang open and he enjoyed the beautiful twin mounds as they moved, glimpses revealed, teasing, tantalizing. She put her hand against his face. "I promise I'll come back" she said. "Not only to tell Conley."

"That's nice," he said blandly.

"You won't be sorry you let me go my way," she said.

"I know that," he said, and saw her eyes narrow a fraction. "Because I'm not letting you go," he finished.

She sat up straighter. "You promised," she accused. "Dammit, you promised."

"You know I didn't promise a damn thing," he protested.

"You said as much. You said it'd make a difference."

"It has. I feel a lot closer to you now, Crystal," Fargo commented.

"Bastard," she roared. "You never intended to let me go."

"Didn't say I did."

She swung, quick as a cat, and he felt the sting of the blow on his face. "Bastard, bastard," she screamed.

He returned the slap and her head spun for a moment.

"You enjoyed it as much as I did, maybe more," he flung at her. "So we're even there."

"You tricked me," she shot back, and he saw the tears hang in her eyes.

He reached out, cupped her face with his hand. "You tricked yourself. You heard what you wanted to hear," he told her, and pulled her to him. "Dammit, why don't you level with me?"

She shook her head into his shoulder, and he lifted her face again, saw the wet marks on her cheeks. But her eyes held stubbornness again. He lay down and pulled her with him. "Better get some sleep. It'll be a hard-riding day tomorrow," he said.

She settled into the crook of his arm and was asleep in minutes. He watched her for a time. Every day she added a new contradiction, but the panic and anxiety were closer to the surface each time. Closer, but not close enough. Something deep held her, a terrible fear or a consuming hate. But he'd been right about one thing he'd told her. It had made a difference. She wasn't simply a beautiful, two-faced little bitch any longer. She was a beautiful enigma, a fascinating package of opposites and still the most beautiful woman he'd ever seen. He closed his eyes and slept, and she felt nice beside him.

He woke first in the new day and washed and made coffee as she got up. She took the cup he offered with truculence, her eyes glowering at him. He let her finish, waited to see if her mood changed, but the glower remained. She rose, started to walk toward her horse when he reached out, spun her around, and pushed her to the ground. His hand cupped one full breast. "Tell me you're sorry about last night," he hissed at her. "Go on, let me hear you say it." She glared up at him, tight-lipped. He pressed his mouth on hers, felt her lips grow soft, answering. When he pulled back, the glower had softened. "Go on, say it," he said again, gentler now.

She looked away as she answered. "I can't. Last night was something special," she said, her voice very small. He let her go, pulled her to her feet.

"Then take that damn pout off your face," he said.

"Go to hell," she snapped, but the pout was gone, replaced by anger. He grinned at her as she climbed onto her horse. He set out across the lower part of the mountain, doubling back the way they'd come. It was dangerous, but he circled back to leave a trail that bisected itself.

"That'll slow Conley for a spell until he unravels it," Fargo commented. Crystal, he saw, watched everything he did with grim unhappiness, but she didn't catch the other things he saw: underbrush just beginning to spring back in place, the thin new twigs of low-hanging branches snapped off. Riders had come this way, at least a half-dozen, he guessed. Too close, he thought. He halted, rested the horses, looked casually at Crystal. "Which way do we go now?" he asked idly.

She frowned at him. "Why ask me all of a sudden?" she said suspiciously.

He shrugged. "Courtesy, my dear. I want you to be happy."

"Hell you do," she said, sniffing.

"No preferences at all?" he asked mildly.

Her eyes narrowed at him. "Very clever. No preferences," she said.

He turned the pinto. "Then we'll drift on toward South Pass," he said offhandedly, but his quick sharp glance caught the flash of hope in her eyes. She'd answered one more question. He'd been right all along. She'd been heading for South Pass. Fargo took a trail that led along the side of the mountains, rid-

117

ing in tight-lipped silence. The signs of the riders gnawed at him. Conley was closer than he should have been, and another thought stabbed at him. Conley may have decided to move boldly. Aware he was onto a fresh trail, he may have sent half his posse racing ahead to turn and work their way back. The plan, of course, to catch the quarry in a pincer or make him turn into one or the other band of pursuers. Fargo's lips thinned as he considered the very real chance of Conley's maneuver. He rode on and let his eyes scan the top of the mountains. He didn't want to head for real high ground—not yet, when they were this close. They could pick up the trail, and high ground decreased maneuverability and afforded less tree cover.

He decided to wait another day to see what more he could pick up before leaving the low foothills. He continued to move in an uneven line, turning into small passages and branching out into others. "You can't keep this up forever," Crystal muttered as the day neared an end.

"No, not forever. Just long enough," he said calmly, smiled at her as she glowered at him. When dark settled over the hills, he found a small ledge of land that looked out across the rolling foothills but afforded a protected, tucked-away little nest. Once again the night stayed warm and he fixed a meal from his rations, cooked over a small fire. Later, Crystal sat and stared into the dancing flames, seemingly wrapped in her own thoughts.

"Thinking about last night?" he slid at her.

Her eyes blinked at him. "Maybe," she said. "But not the way you're thinking."

"Oh?"

"I was thinking it's not going to happen again, not unless you promise to let me go," she said.

"No matter how much you want?" he asked,

reaching out to let his hand move along the side of her neck, down to the soft skin over her breastbone.

"It's a matter of principle, not wanting," she said. "Or wouldn't you know about that?" She snapped the remark at him. "You probably don't think much about anything except your own wants," she added haughtily.

"That's pretty much right," he said calmly. "Once in a while I make an exception. But only once in a while."

He stood up, started to kick dirt over the fire. "It'll be interesting, won't it?" he remarked, saw her frown up at him. "Our sleeping in the small bedroll. I guess we'll see how much principle has it over wanting."

"We certainly will see," she said stiffly, and he smiled as he turned away, walked to the small line of brush that closed off the little ledge. She was working hard to convince herself, he reflected. He stood for a moment and let his eyes rove across the dark silhouettes of the foothills as they dipped and rose under a half-moon. Suddenly he felt his body stiffen. A soft-orange glow rose up behind one of the dark, distant ridges, the penumbra of a campfire. His eyes watched the glow as questions raced through his mind. Conley and all of the posse? Or only part of his men? Were they just camping down for the night or waiting for others? If he could find out, it'd decide his moves in the morning. It'd be worth the risk. Not all that much of a risk under cover of night. His eyes measured the distance to the orange glow. Not more than an hour's ride in the darkness, he guessed, maybe only half an hour. He turned, his decision made, walked back to where Crystal had slipped on another nightshirt from her saddlebag.

"I've some other finding out to do," he told her.

"We've got company not too far away. I'm going to have a closer look."

She didn't answer, watched him as he went to the pinto and took the lariat. "I won't go anywhere," she said.

"You wouldn't think of it," he remarked. "I won't be gone long."

She started to move backward, but he reached out, pulled her arms forward. "Take the horse with you," she said. "I certainly can't go far on foot in the dark."

"Far enough," he said, starting to wrap the lariat around her wrists, putting both hands behind her back. Finished, he bent down and tied her ankles.

"Talk about last night? It didn't mean anything at all to you, obviously," she said.

"Not this much," he conceded. He lifted her, put her down on the ground against a tree trunk. His hands lifted the nightshirt, moved along the cleavage between the full, ripe breasts. "Just making sure this time," he said. She glared at him. He pulled the kerchief from his back pocket, started to twist it into a gag, and the glare became astonishment.

"You're not. You wouldn't," she gasped.

"Wrong again," he said. "I'm not having you start to scream after I get there. Sound can carry a helluva distance in these hills at night."

"Anything could happen to me while you're away and I'll be helpless. I couldn't even scream," she protested, her eyes filled with rage. "Some animal, a bear, maybe, could come."

"Damn unlikely," Fargo said. "Besides, if a bear did come nosing around, you'd be better off for not being able to scream. I'm doing you a favor."

"Bastard. You're a rotten bastard, Fargo," she raged. "You don't have to do this. You're just being—" The rest of the sentence became a muffled

120

gasp as he pushed the gag into her mouth and tied it behind her.

He bent over, kissed her cheek. "Simmer down. I'll be back soon enough," he said. He rose, swung onto the pinto, looked back at her. Her eyes were thin black coals of fury and she was making muffled sounds under the gag, none of them complimentary, he was certain. "You can blame yourself," he commented. "You could've been on your way." The muffled sounds rose from beneath the gag and her eyes blazed as he wheeled the pinto around and rode off.

The half-moon cast a dim light in the heavily wooded places and he found his pace slowed until he came out below. He quickened his pace then, rode on till he began to climb the slope of the next row of foothills. The orange glow had grown dimmer, just barely enough edging the ride for him to follow. He rode till he saw the glow begin to take on strength again, dismounted, and led the pinto on foot into a line of Norway spruce, threading his way through the tall, fresh-scented trees. The murmur of voices drifted toward him and he dropped the pinto's reins over a low branch and crept forward. He moved to the top of the ridge line and ducked down at once. The campsite was not down in a hollow as he'd expected but lay directly in front of him, the land leveling off in a small plateau.

He scanned the figures grouped around the fire, six in all. Not one wore a deputy's badge, he noted, frowning. A thin, sallow-faced man in the center seemed to be top hand by the way the others listened to him.

"Goddamn, we've got to find her," he heard the man say. "Tomorrow we move up into the mountains."

"She didn't come in through the Oregon Trail,

121

Jed, or we'd have seen her moving up the pass," a man with a red kerchief said.

"I know, and that bothers me," the one called Jed answered. "She should've been coming that way."

Fargo's eyes narrowed. Not Conley's men, none of them. They looked for Crystal, not him.

"Why'd the boss send us out looking for her?" The red kerchief said. "She's headin' back anyway."

"To make sure nobody else gets hold of her. We find her and bring her back safe. He'll see to the rest," Jed said.

Fargo felt his frown dig deeper into his forehead. The man's words had a strange note in them, something unsaid. He found himself wondering if Crystal knew what she was racing back to with such bitter determination. His eyes moved over the men again. They were one more problem, and Conley was enough. He measured the position of each man, decided he could take out most of them with one burst. He was still turning the possibilities over in his mind when he felt a cold round object press into his spine. "Don't move, mister," the voice said. He saw the others look up from the campfire, felt the hand reach down and pull the big Remington from its holster. The pistol barrel was pulled back from his spine. "Now get up and start walking," the voice said.

Fargo obeyed, cursing silently. The others were on their feet as he walked into the circle of firelight. The man behind him stepped to the side, a watery-eyed face behind a Colt .45 that didn't waver. "Look here what I found, Jed," he said. "Right over the ridge, listenin' and lookin'."

The sallow-faced one moved toward him and Fargo kept his expression bland.

"I always told you it was good to take a walk before turning in," the watery-eyed one chortled.

122

"Who are you, mister?" the sallow-faced man barked.

"Jones. Sam Jones," Fargo answered easily. Anything to identify him was in his saddlebag.

"You always come sneaking around other people's fires?" the man asked.

"I saw the fire and came to have a look. I thought it might be Arapaho," Fargo said mildly.

"What're you doin' out here?" Jed asked.

"Riding the trail," Fargo said.

"You're a good ways off the Oregon Trail, mister," the man barked. "You giving us a story?"

"Why'd I do that?" Fargo asked back.

"You tell me," the man growled.

"No reason to." Fargo shrugged, let his eyes flick to the others.

"I don't like it," the one with the red kerchief said. "He don't look like no ordinary saddlebum."

"We take him back to Malloy?" the watery-eyed one said.

"Shut up," the leader barked, spun on the man. "Close your big mouth."

Fargo let his face stay unmoved while he filed the name in his mind. *Malloy*, he repeated silently. They worked for somebody named Malloy.

The sallow-faced man had returned his eyes to Fargo, peered sharply at the tall black-haired man. "I think you're lying, cousin," he said. "And we're goin' to find out why."

The man started toward him, halted, frowned as he cocked his head to one side. Fargo had already caught the sound, hoofbeats rumbling through the night, and he cursed silently. He wasn't the only one who'd seen the fire's glow. The sallow-faced man turned to the others. "Maybe he's got friends," he murmured. "Take him off a ways and keep him

123

quiet till we see who the hell's coming. Gag the bastard."

Fargo's face remained expressionless, but he had a damn good notion who the approaching horsemen were. The one with the red kerchief took it off and wrapped it around the Trailsman's mouth. Fargo felt himself pushed forward, propelled up behind the ridge where he had hidden. He was pushed farther back into the darkness, higher up on the ridge, then spun around and flung facedown on the ground. The cold end of the gun barrel came against his temple. "One move and you've got no head left," the man growled.

Fargo lay still, his eyes on the campfire below, and silently cursed his luck. His chance had been exploded because one stupid bastard had been off walking about. He let his arm stretch down to his leg. He could just feel the edge of the leg holster that held the knife. Carefully, he pulled the trouser leg up, working it slowly, gathering the material with his fingers. The sound of the hooves grew louder and he saw the riders come into view, move into the circle of firelight. Bloodhound Conley's ramrod figure sat astride the lead horse, his voice carrying clearly beyond the ridge.

"Sheriff's posse," the man barked. "I'm Sheriff Conley."

The man called Jed nodded. "What can we do for you, Sheriff?" he asked.

"We thought your fire might belong to the man we're after," Conley said.

"Who's that?" the man asked.

"Name's Fargo . . . Skye Fargo," Conley said. "Big, tall buster, black hair and blue eyes. He'd most likely be with a fine-looking, red-haired young woman."

Fargo saw the sallow-faced man exchange looks with the others. He heard the soft whisper from just beyond the gun at his temple. "Well, dammit now. What do you know?" The whisper half-chuckled. He felt the gun barrel jammed harder into his temple. "Soon as that lawman leaves, Jed will be wanting to talk more with you, Mr. Fargo," the voice hissed.

The Trailsman's fingers continued to gather the trouser leg up and now he could feel the leather of the holster, the tip of the knife handle. Below, he watched Jed squint up at Conley. "Fargo, you say? And you think he's in these parts?" the man questioned.

"He's here. We keep picking up the trail, then losing it," Conley said. "I've two men at the Oregon Trail, where the pass through the mountains starts. If you see them, I'd be obliged you send someone down to tell my men there."

"Sure thing, Sheriff," Jed said.

Fargo watched as Conley took his men off, riding quickly away into the night, the others waiting motionless till the posse was out of sight.

"Get up, Fargo," the man at his side ordered and he felt the gun pulled back from his temple. Fargo started to lift himself to his feet, moving slowly, his hand closing around the handle of the knife on his leg. As he started to straighten up, he exploded into silent, savage motion. He spun and slashed upward with the knife, plunging it deep into the man's abdomen. With his other hand, he tore the gun from the man as the latter pitched forward, eyes wide, his mouth open, gasping for breath. Fargo pulled the knife back, and the figure fell forward at his feet, a single, long, gasping breath sliding into the night, a final breath.

Fargo crouched down. Below, the sallow-faced

125

man turned, squinted up to the ridge. "Harry," he called out, "bring that son of a bitch down here."

Fargo scooted backward, rose to his feet, and ran, heading up the ridge. "Harry?" he heard the man call again. Dimly, he heard the scramble of footsteps and muffled oaths as they realized something had gone wrong. Fargo crossed down the high part of the ridge, running hard yet silently, down along the far side, then swerved again to move up the slope to where he'd left the pinto. He missed the feel of his big Remington at his side, but he dared not risk trying to retrieve it. He kept running and felt a little as though he were deserting an old and faithful friend. The line of spruce reached out with their fragrance and he darted into the trees, reached the pinto, and swung into the saddle. He held back from galloping off, walked the horse till he was safely out of hearing distance, and then broke into a gallop.

They'd fan out some, he knew, but wait for daylight before setting off on a thorough search. That didn't concern him. If Conley hadn't been able to pick up a clear trail yet, they wouldn't have much luck. But together, Conley's posse and these, things would be getting too crowded. He'd set off for higher ground in the morning. He rode back up the other side of the hills, finally reached the protected little ledge. Crystal's eyes shot fire at him as he dismounted. She had squirmed and kicked herself a half-dozen yards away from the tree, but she was still firmly bound and gagged.

He knelt down, untied her ankles, took the gag from her, and then undid the wrist ropes. She spun like a tigress, clawing at his face, and he barely avoided her nails, rolled to one side. "Damn bastard," she screamed. "Leaving me tied and gagged. Rotten bastard." She scooped up a piece of

126

half-charred wood from the fire and swung it at his head. Once again he ducked, but this time he came up under the blow, seized her arm, and twisted, flung her forward. She fell, the wood flying from her grip. He went after her, but she whirled, kicked out, and he just managed to take the blow on his thigh. "Bastard. You'd no need to do that," she flung at him, half-crying, half-screaming. He blocked another furious blow and caught her arm, pushed her backward, came down half atop her.

"Stop it, you little hellcat," he ordered. She lifted her head, tried to bite his hand, and he pulled her arm down. He pressed his face down on hers, found her lips, kissed her hard, forcing her mouth open. She squirmed, made little noises, and his hand found her breast, cupped it, rubbed briskly across the nipple. He felt her lips tighten, then soften. She tried to twist her legs; he grabbed one, pushed it to one side, and got his hand hard against the soft-wire bush. She was still fighting and he felt his own anger take hold. He got his leg against hers, pushed again, opening her thighs. He was feeling the stiffness inside him, now outside as he unbuttoned trousers, thrust himself over her, just at the entranceway.

"Goddamn you," he murmured. "You want it this way?"

Her eyes were round black coals looking up at him, her breath harsh, short gasps. He moved, pressed his tip against the opened lips, felt the warm wetness. Anger and fury worked the same for her, he realized. Suddenly her arms slid around his neck and she reached her mouth up again, this time her tongue answering. He relaxed his grip on her, drew his breath in, and suddenly, taking him by complete surprise, she bit at him and her hand came up, smashed into the side of his face. She got a knee up

127

into his groin and he flung himself sideways. Her fists were pounding at him.

"No, damn you, no. I'm not giving you a damn thing," she was shouting. "You want it, you take it, you bastard."

He felt the surge of fury spiral through him. His arm came up, warded off her blows, and he caught her shoulder, pressed hard, felt his fingers dig deep. She screamed in pain, fell back, her legs open. He fell onto her, thrusting into her at once, moving with furious strokes. She matched his every movement, her hands grasping at his shoulders, his neck, pulling his head down to her breasts. He felt her contract, close around him, hold tight as the thrustings quickened, but then she screamed into his shoulder, a wild cry of pleasure and relief, and she clung to him as the last ripple of ecstasy filled her. Finally she fell back, breathing deep drafts of air. He raised himself on one elbow beside her, his hand moving gently now across the stiffened little pink tips of her breasts. Her deep, dark eyes half-glowered at him.

"You wanted it that way," he said.

"Did I?" she returned.

"It wasn't rape and you know it. You wanted it to be rape, but it wasn't," he said.

"What was it?" she asked, sitting up.

"Your redheaded temper. Wanting and not wanting. A lot of things all mixed up together. For both of us," he said.

The glower went away. "I guess so," she said quietly, her eyes finding sudden warmth, almost a smile. "But it was good, wasn't it?" she added.

"Yes, a different kind of good," he agreed.

The hint of a pout returned to her face. "You shouldn't have gagged me," she muttered.

He leaned over, pressed his mouth on hers. "I'm going to gag you again," he murmured.

"Yes," she whispered, and this time it was less turbulent, less seething, but no less wonderful. She slept in his arms when they finished, until the day came and he watched her gather her clothes, go behind the brush to change. Modesty had its own funny ways. He laughed quietly.

He'd washed, dressed, and had the coffeepot on over a few embers when she reappeared, hair flashing in the sun. He handed her the single metal cup of the strong brew and she sipped it, made a face, but continued sipping. "What's you find last night?" she asked.

"People out looking for you," he said. "Not just Conley's posse."

"Yes, I expect so," she said thoughtfully. He thought of the remarks that he'd heard, the unsaid something that had bothered him and clung to disturb him. He looked at Crystal and wondered if what she expected and what waited her were one and the same thing.

"Who's Malloy?" he asked, and saw her eyes snap wide, then retreat behind a veil.

"Nobody," she said.

"Isn't it time you stopped playing games and told me the truth?" he asked.

"I'm not playing games," she shouted, instant fury in her eyes.

"All right, I take that back," he said, and her eyes softened. "But it's time you leveled with me." She looked into the coffee and he studied her for a moment. "I think you're in some kind of trouble," he said. "Dammit, maybe I could help."

She shook her head. "I can't go on that," she said. "I don't know what you'd do or say. Neither do you. I just know what I have to do."

"And that means keeping your pretty little mouth

129

shut and keeping my neck just about in a noose," he speared.

"I'm sorry, Fargo," she said, looking up at him. "Just let me go and I'll take care of everything. I'll come back." She put the cup down, came to him, rested her face against his chest. "You know I'll come back, you know that now. God, I know it. You must, too."

He lifted her face up, looked into the deep, liquid eyes. "I know you'd try," he said softly. "But it's not your world."

"Don't you ever take a chance on anybody?" she asked despairingly.

"Sometimes. I don't like the odds on this one," he told her. "Like I said, it's not your world."

She turned away, and when she looked back, anger mingled with tears that refused to be held back. "I hate you, Fargo. You're everything I said last night. You're a real rotten bastard."

"That's me," he snapped. "But without this bastard you'd be a trophy on an Arapaho tepee."

"Maybe you should have left me there for all the good I'm doing this way," she said, sobbing, turned from him, and he watched her wipe her sleeve across her eyes. But the soft sobs continued and her shoulders shuddered. He walked to the row of bushes, gazed out at the hills, morning gold and green now. "Damn her beautiful little ass," he swore. She'd lied about him, tried to run from him, trick him, almost got herself scalped, fought with him and fucked with him, hated him and wanted him, and still she refused to tell him what he wanted to know. Something very deep kept her lips sealed. But now she had added something more, damn her. She'd managed to reach him. He admired guts, the strength not to give in to compromise, an inner hardness that refused to back down. It was a rare quality and she had a big piece of it. Despite what he'd told her, time wasn't all his. Time was making a loser out of both of them. That was plain in the anguish in her eyes.

Yet letting her go was too goddamn risky. Too many thorns sticking out all over this one. He had to make some move, something to break the deadlock. He turned back to her. "Get your things together," he said crisply. "We're going upland."

She looked at him, her eyes dry, protest in them now. "You said we'd drift toward South Pass."

"Changed my mind," he said. "Too much chance of company on the way." Her lips compressed as she strode to her horse. She followed him as he started to climb up the mountainside. He cast a glance below. He didn't pick up any signs from this distance, but they were down there, searching. He turned thoughts from the pursuers. He had to find a way to move Crystal off dead center. He rode wrapped in silence, very aware of her beside him, all the pain and anger in her, the hating and the wanting. She was more than a beautiful contradiction now. She was beauty torn apart inside. He had to figure out something.

7

It was midday and he'd discarded one idea after another when it came to him, the way a horse goes into a box stall—backward. He'd been wondering whether, if he hadn't caught her, she'd have returned one day on her own to tell Conley the truth. Or would she have gone on trying to forget a dead man's innocence on her conscience. It was an idle thought that had run through his head, but it reined up there, refused to leave, and suddenly the rest just backed into place. He turned the plan over as it formed itself, grunted silently at it. He'd be playing the thin edge of the coin. If he was guessing wrong about Crystal, or if too much that was unexpected happened, he'd be handing himself to Conley. He pondered awhile longer. He glanced over at Crystal. No anger in the lovely, deep eyes now, no truculence. Only a haunted pain. To hell with the risks, he muttered silently. He'd go with the damn idea.

He rode on, eyes searching the ground while his nostrils sniffed the air. As usual with the vine, he smelled its sweetness before he reached it. He halted as he came to the nest of brown-purple flowers, nestling near a small stream. "Let's rest here a spell," he said, swinging down excitedly. He went to the bank of flowers and began to pull the vines up by hand, aware of Crystal's eyes on him. "Groundnuts," he said. "Terrific eating, and they'll save our rations," he told her. "They're supposed to be very good for you, too." He pulled at the roots until he drew out the tuberlike bulbs, each about the size of an egg. He sat down, used his knife to peel the surface of each, then cut off small pieces.

"Want some?" he asked, holding one out to her.

"Not hungry," she said, looked faintly distasteful as he chewed the tuber with relish.

"They taste a little like a turnip," he commented. "They're better cooked, but we haven't time for that."

"I hope you know what you're doing," she remarked. "I don't trust raw things much."

He chuckled. "Well, if they're not ripe, I hear they can really do things to you, but I think these are ripe. Don't really know for sure. Never tasted the unripe ones." He continued to chew on the root; she sank to the ground and stretched out as he continued to chew on the plant, let her watch him enjoy it. Finished, he rose, reached a hand out to help her up. She ignored it and pulled herself up. He shrugged and returned to the saddle, set out again. He let a half hour go by until he suddenly reined up, made a face. "Hold it," he said. He grimaced again, put a hand to his stomach. "Jesus," he muttered, and slid from the saddle, motioned for her to dismount. He leaned against the horse until she did, then walked stiffly to a tree, sank down against it. He held his hands to his stomach, put his head back.

"What is it?" she asked, moving to him.

"My stomach. It hurts bad," he said, doubling over. "My canteen . . . get me some water," he mumbled.

She fetched the canteen, opened it for him, and he drank, leaned back against the tree again.

"Those damn roots," she said.

"Not ripe, I guess," he muttered, his eyes half-closed. He took another sip of the canteen, leaned back again. It was a damn good performance, he reflected. "I feel dizzy. Everything's spinning," he gasped out, closed his eyes.

"Fargo, can you hear me?" she asked, concern in her voice. "Are they poisonous?"

"No," he said weakly. "Not poisonous. Narcotic . . . put you to sleep." He let his head fall back, then slid to one side and fell to the ground, his breathing heavy. "Need to sleep . . . sleep . . ." he murmured, his eyes closed. He let his breathing slow, grow even. He felt her sitting there, moving, bending over him. She put her head to his chest, listened to his heart, drew back. She stayed, not moving, and he feigned a deep sleep. She stayed so long that he began to think the idea wasn't going to work. Then he heard her get up, move away. He heard other sounds he couldn't pinpoint and he let his eyes open a slitted fraction. She was tethering the pinto. He closed his eyes instantly as she turned and came over to him again. He felt her kneel down beside him, her hand touch his cheek, a gentle caress. He continued his even, deep breathing.

"I'm sorry, Fargo. I'll come back. I'll go to Conley," she said. "Believe in me when you come about. I won't forget you." She leaned forward, and he felt her lips on his forehead, soft as a butterfly's wings, then the sound of her rising quickly, hurrying away. He heard her swing onto the horse and ride off, opened his eyes just in time to glimpse the flash of flame hair against the dark green of the woods.

He waited a few moments longer, then rose and swung onto the pinto. Following her trail was no task now, and he stayed close enough yet careful to remain out of sight. He let the pinto move alongside thick underbrush, snap off branches. No more setting cross trails for Bloodhound Conley. He'd give the sheriff a beacon he couldn't help but see.

Crystal headed back to the main section of the Oregon Trail where it cut through the mountains, just as he'd expected she would. South Pass lay on the other side of the mountains, and beyond South Pass, the real killer of men and wagons, the towering Tetons. But she'd not go that far, he was wagering. She'd turn off at South Pass, north or south to where the land grew gentler, to whatever waited for her there. She rode hard and he stayed back of her, continued to leave a clear and easy trail of his own. When night fell, she halted and drew into the trees at the side of the trail. He did the same and caught the welcome hours of sleep. He was in the saddle and waiting as she emerged in the dawn, started off again. He'd left the remains of coffee seeds on the ground where he'd made camp. Conley would spot them, he knew. The sheriff would take grim satisfaction in the signs that told him his quarry was getting careless.

Fargo rode on, taking higher ground that let him see glimpses of Crystal as she reached the end of the cut through the mountains. He saw the riders coming toward her before she did, let himself draw closer as she halted. The riders, six of them now, came to a stop beside her, and he picked out the sallow-faced one at once. He smiled quietly to himself. They had searched for him, of course, then decided that he hadn't caught up to her yet and broke off the searching to ride on to the far end of the mountain cut to wait. He wached as Crystal spoke to them for a few moments and then spurred her horse on. The riders fell in on each side of her and he moved after them.

He hung back, watched as Crystal turned off the trail and headed south, the others going with her.

He followed, kept his trail to one side so the hoof-prints would stay clear, turned south after the others. Crystal led them at a fast pace, hurrying the horse, riding the way you ride when you're nearing your goal. She never glanced behind her and neither did the others. He watched them disappear beyond a rise in the land, and when he crested it, he saw the long, low-roofed ranch house in the distance. He halted as Crystal and the others rode up to the house and drew out of clear vision. Dismounting, he backed behind the rise. A thick stand of shade trees fanned out from the ranch house, he noted, and three smaller outbuildings and stables brought up the rear of the house.

He glanced at the sun. Another hour would bring darkness. He sank down on the ground to wait. His eyes continued to scan the distant house. It had started there, all of it, he was certain. And it would end there. Fitting. His hand went down to the holster and drew out the Colt .45. He made a face and wished for the big Remington in his hand. The Colt was a good gun and he sighted the weapon, turned it in his hand. He just wasn't used to it. It took time and practice to get the feel of a gun for accurate shooting. He returned the Colt to the holster. He'd have to make do with it, he grunted, settled down to wait for the night. His eyes returned to the distant ranch house. She was inside. Doing what? he wondered.

He let the night come before rising to look back, first. He'd left the trail for Conley and he half-smiled grimly. Positions had undergone an about-face. Now he was hoping the sheriff and his posse would pick up the trail quickly. It was but one of the pieces in the dangerous game he'd set in motion. He'd lose if the pieces didn't all come together at the right time. Or if he was guessing wrong. He rose, dropped his kerchief just back of the rise. If Bloodhound Conley played his part right, he'd be sure to spot it. Fargo started over the rise, leading the pinto in a wide circle until he reached the far end of the shade trees. Inside their dark protection, he moved toward the ranch house from the side. As he drew closer, he saw three cowhands drift into the bunkhouse. He moved on a little closer, left the pinto, and went on alone. Lights were on in the ranch house, wide-open windows indicating the living room. The tree cover extended close to the open windows and he dropped to his knees, crept close enough to see inside.

It was a large room with Indian weavings. Crystal sat on a leather sofa and another woman sat in a deep chair opposite her. A third figure in the room, by the door, was the sallow-faced man called Jed. Fargo's eyes went to the other woman, not much older than Crystal, but black-haired, a lush body in a black dress, attractive with gray, restless, prowling eyes. She had a pumalike, coiled-spring quality to her. There was tension in the room, evident in Crystal's set face, her hand nervously moving in her lap. The man was something more than an observer, Fargo was certain.

"You said he'd be back by now," Fargo heard Crystal accuse. The other woman shot her a cold glance. "Malloy knew I was on the way," Crystal added, a little petulantly.

Fargo's eyes narrowed, the name now familiar. He saw the other one spit dismissal at Crystal. "He's been waiting," she said. "He had things to do."

Fargo's eyes were watching the black-haired woman, large breasts pressing the black dress out tightly, marking the round points of her nipples. She rose, went to a cabinet, and poured herself a bourbon. She drank from the glass, contempt in her eyes as she glanced at Crystal. The lush, prowling-cat quality of her was sensuous and hard, he decided. She had just returned to her chair with the drink when he heard the sound of horses approaching. He drew back into the trees as four riders came up to halt at the front door of the house. One dismounted and went inside, the others going on to the corral. Fargo crept forward, lifted himself up again to see into the room. The man had just entered, square-faced with hard dark eyes, a wide, flat nose, and a thin line for a mouth. In his forties, trim, a lean body under the shirt and vest he wore.

The black-haired woman draped herself over him at once and he held her with his arm around her waist as his eyes stayed on Crystal. "Took you long enough to get back," he said.

"I had delays," Crystal said.

The lush woman continued to drape around the man, one hand rubbing the side of his neck.

"What kind of delays?" he asked Crystal. "Fargo?"

"For a while," she said. "But I'm here and it's done with, finished. It went just the way you planned, Malloy."

"Hell it did," the man threw back. "Fargo should've been hung in a day. Instead he broke out."

"That's not my fault," Crystal protested.

"Not mine, either, but it's not done this way, not with him running around looking for you," Malloy said.

"He doesn't know anything. I kept my part of the deal. Now you keep yours," Crystal said, her voice rising.

The man glowered at her. "You giving me orders?"

The black-haired woman's hand ran down Malloy's neck. "Don't let her talk to you like that, honey," she said.

Crystal was on her feet instantly, her redheaded temper exploding. "I did my part. You promised me, Malloy. You let him go now, tonight," she said. "I finished my part of it."

"It's not finished. I want to think about it overnight," Malloy answered.

"Dammit, Malloy, you promised. You made a bargain, and you'll damn well stick by it," she snapped, starting toward the man. His blow, openhanded but hard, caught her across the face, to send her stumbling back into the couch.

"Nobody talks to me like that, especially you," the man roared, and Fargo saw the black-haired woman laughing. Malloy gestured to the other man. "Take her away. See that she stays put until tomorrow morning."

The sallow-faced man reached out, grasped hold of Crystal's arm, and yanked her forward with him as he started from the room. Crystal went with one hand held to the side of her face. Fargo didn't move, but he watched the windows down the side of the house until he saw one light at the far end. He returned his eyes to the room where the black-haired woman had pressed herself against Malloy as he sank onto the couch.

"That's what you should've done to her long ago," she murmured, kissing Malloy's face, running her lips down along the side of his neck.

"I couldn't. We needed her," Malloy said.

"But not anymore," the woman said.

"Most likely not," Malloy answered.

The woman frowned at him but continued to stroke his face and nuzzle him. "Most likely not?" she queried.

"That Fargo running around loose. I can't have that. I might need her yet," the man said.

"The honey to attract the bear," the woman said.

139

"Exactly," Malloy said, pressed the woman to him. "After it's done with for good, you can have anything you want . . . anything, honey." The woman continued to stroke his face, run her hands down his chest. Fargo watched with his eyes narrowed. "You're everything to me, Denise. You know that," the man murmured.

"Yes, I know it," she said, pressed herself against him.

Fargo's eyes lingered on the man's face. Malloy wasn't just giving her sweet talk. The woman had him in her grip. In his face there was a mixture of worship, admiration, and lust. Fargo pushed back from the edge of the window, taking careful note of what he'd just witnessed. It could spell the difference, he reflected as he moved along the side of the house to the very end where he'd seen the window light go on. He reached it just in time to see Crystal reach to turn off the lamp in a small, narrow room with faded wallpaper. She was still fully clothed, and as she turned the lamp off, he saw her lie down on a cot along the wall. He waited and the sounds drifted to him through the closed window, hard, bitter sobs half-muffled against a pillow. He waited till they stopped and she found sleep. He reached up, pressed against the window frame to lift it. The window refused to move, locked securely.

He moved away, in a bent-low lope, around the back of the house. The rear door beckoned, a half-dozen steps away but beyond the protection of the trees. He let his eyes scan the bunkhouse area and the corral. No one moved except the horses inside the fences. He reached the door in four running strides, turned the handle, and felt it open. A hallway led along the side of the house, darkened, a faint glow of lamplight at the end. He moved on silent steps to the end of the hall, squatted down, and peered around the corner. The sallow-faced man stood outside the door of the room, leaning against the wall. A small wall lamp afforded flickering light.

Fargo drew the Colt, took the barrel in his hand. Slowly, he scraped his feet along the floor to make a strange, scratching sound. He rose, heard the man's steps coming at once. Fargo struck as the sallow-faced man came around the edge of the corner, his blow catching the man in the middle of his forehead. The heavy butt of the Colt opened his head in a rush of blood and he pitched forward. Fargo brought the gun down once more on the back of his head as he fell; he stepped over him and darted to the room. He pressed the door open carefully, closed it behind him. He heard the steady sound of Crystal's breathing as he stepped to the cot, reached down, and put his hand over her mouth. She snapped awake at once, fright in her eyes, and the fright became surprise as she saw him. He pulled his hand away from her mouth. "Fargo," she gasped.

"Come on, you're getting out of here," he said. Her hand clutched at his arm.

"No, I can't," she whispered. "Not till morning."

He hissed words at her. "Morning, hell. You're going now."

Her hand tightened on his arm. "I can't. I can't run yet. I have to wait till morning."

"Forget what Malloy said," Fargo told her and she frowned at him. "Yes, I heard him, but he's feeding you shit. Whatever your deal was, it's no more. He isn't going to keep it."

She stared at him, panic moving into her eyes again. She clutched at him again. "Will you help me, Fargo?" she asked.

"That's what I'm trying to do, dammit," he returned.

She shook her head. "No, will you help me get my father?" she asked.

"Your father?" Fargo gasped out.

She nodded vigorously. "That's why I did it, all of it. Malloy's holding him," she began.

Fargo stopped her. "Wait, you can't give me all of it here. Let's get out of here first."

"Not without my father," she refused adamantly.

"Where is he? Where's Malloy got him?"

"An old stone storehouse a dozen yards behind the bunkhouse," Crystal said.

"All right, let's go," Fargo said, and she swung out of bed and followed him to the door. He opened it and froze. Four guns pointed directly at him, Malloy holding one, three cowhands the others.

"Come out nice and slow, mister," the man said. "Hands in the air."

Fargo moved forward, raised his hands. Crystal came to stand beside him and one of the cowhands moved forward, took the Colt out of his holster. Malloy's smile was thin. "Lucky I came up to talk to Jed, wasn't it?" he remarked. "You've got to be Fargo."

"You get the cigar," the Trailsman said grimly.

"I didn't expect you this soon," the man said. He waved the gun, gestured to the cowhands. "Take him into the living room. Her, too."

Fargo lowered his hands as the men pushed him along the hallway and around a corner, down to the room he'd seen from outside the window. The woman, Denise, gazed at him with eyes narrowed, her gaze traveling up and down his body. Malloy came in, faced him again, the smile still thin, a pleased, self-satisfied expression in it.

"We got lucky, honey," Malloy said to her, reached an arm around her waist.

"Who the hell are you, Malloy?" Fargo asked. "What's all this about?"

142

"What's it about? It's about paying back old debts," Malloy said. "It's about paying back a righteous bastard for fifteen years of my life."

"Kent?" Fargo offered.

"That's right, Kent," the man bit out, his face growing harsh. "I came up before him when he was a judge, a long time back. He could've given me half-a-dozen sentences. He gave me the longest time in the hardest place. I swore I'd get even one day."

"And me?" Fargo questioned.

"You fitted right," the man said. "For fifteen years I planned ways to get him, but they all had something wrong with them. Then I got the idea after I was out."

"After he saw me," Crystal cut in bitterly.

"That's right." Malloy smiled. "I had to get Kent without putting myself out on a limb again. The first thing was to stay far away so there'd be no chance anybody could tie me into what was going on. I did a few jobs and got this place for myself. The second thing was to drive Kent off his land, ruin him. I got to a lot of his suppliers, but too many others kept hanging in with him."

"So you decided on killing him," Fargo said. "But with a murderer all supplied for it."

"That's right. I'd heard about you. I remember when your old man and the family were killed. There was talk then of how you and Kent had words over it. You fitted perfect."

"And Crystal?"

"I needed someone inside to tell what happened, someone everybody'd believe. Of course, the first thing was for her to become the new Mrs. Howard Kent. I didn't figure he'd take too long to hold out. I was right, too," Malloy said. "It all went off damn near perfect."

"Except for my breaking out of Bloodhound Conley's jail," Fargo said.

The man nodded agreement. "Except for that," he said. "And now that's all settled up."

"We had a bargain, Malloy," Crystal blurted.

His laugh was harsh. "That's right, we *had* one, gorgeous, but it's over, for you and for your pa." He turned to fasten a narrowed stare at the Trailsman. "Only thing I have to do is to decide how I can get the most out of getting rid of you. I hear Bloodhound Conley's looking hard for you. It might be the best thing just to turn you over to him all legal like." He paused for a moment. "I want to think some on it," he muttered.

"Stinking, rotten liar," Fargo heard Crystal yell, her flame-haired temper exploding as she flew at Malloy, clawing and kicking. The man ducked instinctively as one of the cowhands grabbed her, knocked her back with a blow to the stomach. Fargo's body tensed, ached to erupt, his eyes flicking to the guns held on him, measuring distances, risks, chances, in one instant glance. It was no good, not yet, the invitation only to suicide. He held himself back, forced his hands to unclench.

"Put them in with the old man for now," Malloy ordered, and Fargo felt the gun shoved into his back. He was taken outside into the night, Crystal falling in step beside him, still drawing her breath back. Two gunslingers walked behind and one on each side, all with guns in hand. Fargo's eyes went out into the darkness, to the rise in the distance. Where the hell was Conley, he pondered.

"I'm sorry, Fargo," he heard Crystal say, her voice low, filled with dullness. "Sorry for everything."

"How did he get hold of your father?" the Trailsman asked as they walked.

"Dad ran a dry-goods store in Sandy Hole. I

helped him in the store. Malloy came in a few times with his woman when she bought material. Then one day he came back with his gunhands and just took us," she told him.

"What the hell made you think he'd let you and your pa go when it was over?" Fargo speared, unable to keep the anger out of his voice.

"I had to go along with him or let him kill my pa. I'd no choice, did I?" she returned.

"No, I guess not," he agreed grimly. "Except you could've told me the truth. I might've figured out something."

"I was afraid. If I did one thing wrong, Malloy said, my father was as good as dead," Crystal answered.

Fargo half-shrugged. It was rotten all around, made worse by fear on her part. He halted as they reached the small stone hut, and one of the gunhands slid back the half-rusted heavy iron bolt on the door, pulled the door open. A rush of stale air billowed out as Fargo followed the girl inside. A lone candle offered a flickering glow and he saw the man rise from a torn mattress, white hair, a drawn, thin face. Crystal ran to him, gathered him in her arms as Fargo heard the door bolted again from outside. She turned to Fargo, her arm linked into the old man's thinness. "My father, Tim Derrigan," she introduced with entirely inappropriate formality.

"Glad you're still alive," Fargo said. He let Crystal fill in the broad outlines of all that had happened, and when she finished, the old man turned his eyes back to Fargo.

"I'm sorry you're into this, young fellow," he murmured. "Sorry for everything Crystal had to do. I'm an old man. I've lived my piece, but you're both young. I told Crystal that, told her to let Malloy go ahead and kill me, but she wouldn't listen. I told her not to believe any deals Malloy offered."

"It's all past history now, Pops," Fargo said. "I tried to put an ace in my sleeve, but it hasn't shown yet."

"An ace?" Crystal frowned.

"Conley," Fargo said. "I left a trail he couldn't miss. But I figured him to show up before now."

"What do you think happened?" she asked.

Fargo made a face. "Something I didn't count on. Conley's too damned smart a tracker. I think he figured the trail I left was a false lead. It'll take him a good spell to decide it wasn't. We can't wait for that any longer."

"Waiting is all we can do," Crystal said glumly.

Fargo reached down, drew the knife from the leg holster. "Maybe not," he said. "The wood of this door is old, dried out. It'll take the night to do it, but I'm sure going to try." He dug into the wood, saw the first chips come out at once, the wood offering little resistance as he gouged deeply with the knife. He began to cut away just under and to one side of where the bolt lay on the other side. It was painfully slow, yet the knife blade made headway. Crystal and her father took turns when he paused to rest his arm. It was nearly dawn when the knife broke through to the outside of the door and Fargo whittled the hole wider, boring into it with twisting, turning motions of the knife. Finally he had it just large enough to get his hand and wrist through. His fingers felt the rusted bolt and he pushed his arm through the hole as far as it would go. His fingers pressed into the bolt and he drew lips back in a grimace of pain as he pulled back on the bolt, lost his precarious grip, then tried again. It took six painful attempts and his fingers were cramping up on him when finally he slid the bolt all the way back.

146

He pulled his hand back inside, rubbed circulation into his wrist and fingers, then pushed the door open a fraction. It was still dark but a thin, gray-blue line lay just over the horizon. "You strong enough to sit a horse on your own?" he asked the old man. Tim Derrigan nodded and Fargo turned to Crystal. "The corral first, then I'll pick up the pinto," he said. She followed him outside, her father behind her. Fargo saw a light come on in the bunkhouse. They'd just be waking, starting to make coffee. He led the way in a loping run, reached the corral gate, and held it open for the old man to enter. A dozen horses pricked their ears up. Crystal got hold of two wearing rope halters, a gray mare and a chestnut one. She pulled too hard and the gray mare let out a loud whinny. Three more took it up instantly.

Fargo dropped to the ground as he saw the bunkhouse door open, two heads poke out, squint at the corral. Tim Derrigan moved backward along the corral fence, squatted down, moved back deeper into the shadows when his foot hit a metal pail. It went over with a clatter that sounded like a cannon going off. "Damn," Fargo swore as the bunkhouse door burst open and a half-dozen cowhands raced out. He saw Crystal's look of panic as he rolled half-under one of the horses, came up behind the others. "Don't get yourself shot trying to run," he hissed, dropped down again, and ran, staying behind the milling animals. He ducked out through the other side of the corral, dived, hit the ground, and rolled into heavy shadows from the house.

He saw the window open and Malloy's head come out. Crystal's voice, a half-scream as they seized her, carried easily to the house. "What the hell is it?" Malloy called out. "What's going on out there?"

Fargo heard the voices call back. "The girl and the old man. They got out. We've got them here."

"Holy shit," Malloy thundered. "Bring 'em in here, goddammit."

Fargo rolled, crawled, slid, finally ran the last few yards to the rear of the ranch house and inside the hallway off the back door.

"Where's Fargo?" he heard Malloy call.

"We ain't got him yet," the answer came.

"Find him, goddammit," Malloy shouted. "Find that big bastard."

Fargo pressed himself against the wall. He could see along the hallway to where Malloy pulled his head back from the window. Denise appeared, a diaphanous nightgown around her, to hand Malloy his trousers. Fargo watched the man draw them on as he cursed, started to run down the hall to the front of the house still fastening his belt.

Fargo moved forward as the woman started to go back inside the bedroom. He quickened his steps, reached the door. She was in the room, standing by the bed, smoothing her hair with her hands. He spun around the edge of the door, the knife in his hand, and she sensed something, whirled to see him. Her eyes widened, surprise and fear, as she saw the blade in his grip.

"What are you doing here?" she said, gasping.

"I have some ideas for you," he told her.

"You're crazy. You'll never get away with it," she said.

"You may be right about the first part, but you're wrong about the second," he said. He moved toward her and she started to shrink back. "No noise, honey. Don't make me do something I don't want to do."

"Jesus, no. Don't hurt me," she said.

"That'll depend on you and lover boy," Fargo answered. His hand shot out, quick as a cougar's slash,

148

grabbed her wrist, and spun her around in front of him. He circled her neck with one hand, holding the knife to her throat. Her rear, full and soft, rested against him through the thin nightgown. She had a good body, softly rounded, firm-fleshed, and warm. "Too bad we haven't more time, honey," he remarked.

She managed to half-turn her head to gaze at him. "Maybe I could find time," she said. "If you give me a chance."

"Nice try," he said. "Start walking, honey. Nice and slow." He moved into the hall with her, steered her toward the front of the house, where Malloy's voice filled the air with fury. He heard the sharp slap and Crystal's cry of pain. "Where is he?" Malloy roared.

"I don't know. He got away, and I'm glad," Crystal shot back. Another slap resounded, followed by another gasp of pain.

"Let her be," Fargo heard Tim Derrigan shout and then the old man's oath as a blow landed on him. Fargo, the knife at Denise's throat, moved to the edge of the living room, glimpsed Crystal and her father with three gunhands and Malloy. The man's back was to him, his neck red in fury. A half-dozen more of Malloy's gunslingers crowded together near the front door to the room.

"Get out there and find that bastard. He can't be far yet," Malloy ordered.

"Not far at all," Fargo said quietly, pushing into the doorway with the woman, the knife against her throat. He saw Malloy spin around, his eyes wide, astonishment first, then fear and alarm. The man's mouth worked once or twice before the words came in a hoarse croak.

"Jesus, let her go, Fargo. Don't cut her," Malloy said.

149

"I'll take her head off if I have to, Malloy," Fargo growled.

"Hurt her and you're dead, Fargo," the man rasped.

"One wrong move and she's dead, Malloy," the Trailsman countered, his eyes ice blue.

"Do what he says," the woman half-whispered. "He's crazy."

"Better listen to her, Malloy," Fargo agreed.

"You can't get away with this, Fargo," the man said, trying to summon courage.

"And you can't stop me from cutting her head off," Fargo said. "Let the girl and her father go and you can have your girlfriend back in one piece."

He saw the man's eyes waver, look at the woman, the others, then return to the grim-faced, black-haired man in front of him. "Your move, Malloy. Hurry up and decide," Fargo said. He pressed the edge of the knife against the woman's throat and she screamed out words at once.

"For Christ's sake do what he wants," she cried.

"They go or she goes, lover boy," Fargo growled, his voice steel. He pressed the blade a fraction more.

"Malloy!" Denise screamed.

The man's eyes held alarm and concern as he looked at the woman, and as Fargo watched, they grew smaller, a frustrated anger taking over their orbs. "All right, Fargo. You win. Let her go," he said.

"When they're on their way. Let them out first. Let them get horses and go," Fargo said. He saw Crystal turn to him, her eyes wide, a protest gathering. He cut it off harshly. "Get out of here, *now*," he barked at her. She moved, her eyes still on him, and the old man went with her. The gunhands backed off as she led her father out of the house. Fargo, dragging Denise with him, keeping her in front of him, moved to the window. Day had come over the land and he could see Crystal, running now, her father behind her, as she reached the corral, took hold of the two horses with the rope halters. She helped her father on one, swung onto the other. As she rode through the corral gate, she looked back at the house for an instant, somehow heard his silent command, spurred the horse into a gallop.

"Now let her go," Malloy's voice rang out. Fargo turned to the man, keeping his hold on Denise. "Let her go," Malloy thundered.

"Not till they've got a good head start, enough so you can't send your dogs out to bring them right back," Fargo said.

"How long is that going to be?" Malloy demanded.

"When I say so. Don't make me nervous. My hand could slip," Fargo said. He moved Denise forward, turning with her, keeping her in front of him, the knife steady against her throat. Malloy watched, his eyes quiet fury, but the fear in the woman's face kept his rage in check.

"Easy, honey. It'll be all right," he told her.

"Sure it will, honey, if lover boy doesn't try anything," Fargo said in her ear. He backed the woman toward the front door, his eyes scanning the others as they followed. "Don't crowd me," he warned.

"Jesus, don't crowd him," Denise shouted agreement.

Fargo held her as he backed out of the door and into the yard outside. He continued to move backward, toward the trees where he'd left the pinto. Malloy followed cautiously, his gunhands behind him. Fargo's eyes narrowed as he ticked off the minutes. Crystal had a fair start now. By the time he maneuvered Denise back to the pinto she'd have another five minutes. It was as much as he could give her. Malloy was on the edge, Fargo realized, wound up tight enough to fly off at any moment. He was nearing the trees when the galloping hooves sounded, coming on fast. He swung to one side, keeping his hold of the woman. The band of horsemen raced into the ranch grounds, the ramrod figure leading the way.

"Shit," Fargo spat out. He moved back as the sheriff reined up, drew his gun. The rest of his posse pulled their guns, too.

Conley's gray eyes riveted on the Trailsman, but he addressed his words to Malloy. "Sheriff's posse," he said, tight-lipped. "We'll take care of him."

Malloy was quick to seize his chance. "He'll kill her. He broke in and grabbed her. He wants money and a horse," the man shouted.

Bloodhound Conley's gray eyes were hard as a wall as he trained the gun on Fargo and the girl. "Looks like this is where I came in, Fargo," he rasped.

"I know it's going to be hard for you to believe this, Conley, but he's lying. He planned the Kent killing," Fargo said. He grimaced inwardly at the truth in his own words.

"You're damn right about being hard to believe, Fargo," the sheriff said, his voice flat. "Let the girl go."

"Dammit, Conley, I know how it looks, but it's not like that. Ask Crystal Kent," Fargo returned.

Conley's voice was quiet, his face stone. "Let the girl go, Fargo, or I'll blast you into next month."

"You'll kill her, too," Fargo reminded him.

"If I have to," the sheriff rasped. "But you're not going anywhere again."

"He's crazy. He'll kill her, Sheriff," Malloy interrupted.

Conley didn't move, his eyes unblinking. "He might. I can't help that, mister, much as I'd like to."

His horse moved a step forward and Fargo saw him draw the hammer back on the big Colt. "Let her go or you're a dead man, Fargo. You can get her killed, too, if you want, but one way or the other you'll be dead."

Fargo peered into the stone-gray eyes. Conley had no emotional attachment to the woman. There was no lever left, nothing to use against Conley. Fargo took the knife away from Denise, stepped back. He was never much for useless sacrifice. "Drop the knife," the sheriff ordered, and Fargo let the blade slip from his fingers. At a gesture, two of the posse swung from their horses, had rope around his wrists in moments.

"God, am I ever grateful to you, Sheriff. It was sure lucky you came along when you did," Malloy said, rushing forward, gathering Denise against him. "Who's this Crystal Kent he was talking about?"

"Another one of his wild stories," Conley said.

"You'll string his neck?" Malloy asked.

"I'll take him back with me and it'll be done proper," the sheriff said. He turned to Fargo. "Where'd you leave your horse?"

"Back there in the trees," Fargo told him, and Conley dispatched a man who returned with the pinto in minutes.

"Get on," Conley ordered. His wrists bound in front of him, Fargo grasped the saddle horn with both hands and pulled himself up. He glanced at Malloy. The man couldn't conceal the glee in his eyes. "Ride," Conley barked, swung in beside Fargo.

"Where the hell were you last night, Conley?" Fargo bit out as they rode over the rise. "Or early this morning?"

"Following your damn trail," the sheriff said. "Making sure I had the right one."

"I didn't kill Kent," Fargo said.

153

"Just ride," Conley ordered, and Fargo lapsed into silence. But only for a few minutes.

"Dammit, Conley, you're one thickheaded man," he exploded. "Crystal Kent and her father aren't that far from here and by now that bastard Malloy is setting out with every gunhand looking to kill them both."

Conley halted, reached over, and pulled the pinto to a stop. He leaned over, drew a pocket knife from his shirt, and severed the wrist bonds. Fargo eyed the man suspiciously.

"I met up with Crystal Kent and her pa on the way here," Conley said. "There was time only to tell me some of it, but it was enough. I had to play it straight back there at Malloy's to get you out alive."

"I'll be damned," Fargo said.

Conley handed him a Colt. "Now let's go back and get that son of a bitch on our terms," the sheriff said.

Fargo took the gun, slipped it into the holster, and wheeled the pinto in a tight circle. "My pleasure, Sheriff," he barked. Bloodhound Conley set off at a gallop, Fargo drawing alongside him, the rest of the posse following close. "I figure Malloy will take his gunslingers west before he splits them into small search parties."

"Just how I figure it," Conley said.

"There's a dip in the land. We can be there waiting for him," Fargo said.

"I'll enjoy that," Conley growled. Fargo rode beside him as they reached the dip in the land covered with low trees and thick brush. They rode to the far end of the saucerlike area, spaced man and horses along the edge. Fargo found himself beside Conley as they waited. "You cover a trail pretty damn good, Fargo," the sheriff commented blandly.

"You chase pretty damn good, Sheriff," Fargo returned, and heard Conley's grunt. "Tell me something, Conley," the Trailsman urged. "Back at Malloy's, you said you'd get me even if it meant killing the woman."

"That's what I said," Conley echoed.

"If you hadn't met Crystal, would it have made any difference back there?" Fargo queried.

"Nope," Conley bit out.

"Didn't think so," Fargo said blandly. The knot of horsemen came into view at the top of the dip, started down into the shallow hollow. Conley raised his arm, held it for a moment, brought it down in a fast motion. The hollow erupted in gunfire and three of the gunhands toppled from their horses. Two more whirled, half-rose in the saddle, and fell to the ground. Fargo had Malloy almost in his sights when the man bolted up the incline. The others had recovered, were returning fire, and Fargo saw Conley and his men riding single file, crosswise, making moving targets of themselves. But his eyes were on Malloy as the man neared the top of the incline. Fargo spurred the pinto up along the other side of the saucer of land, came over the top, and raced along the perimeter. He closed the ground between himself and Malloy at an angle, saw the man glance back at him, let a wild shot go, which Fargo ignored.

Fargo let the pinto full out, closed the distance to Malloy quickly, still coming at him at almost a right angle. Malloy lay low over the horse's neck, seemed bent on running and nothing else. The sound of gunfire behind him began to diminish, the attack quick and effective. Fargo urged the pinto forward, using both hands on the reins, closed the space between himself and Malloy. The man didn't look back at all as he fled, and then, entirely unexpectedly, he reined up in a cloud of dust, whirled, and began to fire a hail of bullets. Fargo dived from the pinto as the shots sprayed the air where he'd been.

155

He hit the ground, rolled over, and came up firing. His first shot hit Malloy in the side and Fargo saw the man clasp his ribs in pain. The second shot struck him full in the chest and he flew across the horse's rump to land on the ground. He half-rose on one elbow, leveled his revolver at Fargo. The Trailsman's gun barked again and the man arched his back in a convex arc, rose for an instant, then collapsed to the ground like some deflated object.

Fargo got to his feet, walked to the still form, stared down at the man. He reached down to the dead man's hand, pulled his big Remington .44 out of the already stiffening fingers. He heard the horse pounding up to where he stood, turned to see Conley and one of his men.

"You all right?" the sheriff asked, and Fargo nodded. "Three of my boys got clipped. None too bad," the sheriff said. "They'll be able to make it back to Pointed Rock to see a proper doctor."

"He doesn't need a doctor," Fargo said of the inert form on the ground. "What about the woman at the ranch?"

"Not important anymore. She'll find her own way," Conley said. "My men will cover these over." He paused, looked down at the still figure. "Don't pay to hold a grudge like he did, eat yourself up for so many years and end up dead."

"There's another lesson," Fargo said.

"What's that?"

"Things aren't always what they seem," he remarked.

Conley's eyes met his for a long moment. "Guess not," the man said evenly.

"Where's Crystal?" Fargo asked.

"Just a ways on past the cedars," the sheriff said, and Fargo turned his horse, rode away. He held to the edge of the cedar stand as it made a slow curve and suddenly he saw her, leaning against a rock. She stood up as he came into view, drew to a halt.

"Where's your pa?" he asked.

"One of the sheriff's men took him back to Sandy Hole. I wanted to wait here. Is it done with?" she asked.

"All of it." He nodded.

Her face was grave. "Rotten, every part of it rotten," she said.

"You're still Mrs. Kent according to law. You've a ranch waiting for you," he said.

She shook her head. "I'll sell it, give it away, maybe. I don't want any part of it. It's not mine really. I'm not living the rest of my life with a lie around my neck."

"That'll take a while to finish up. What are you going to do now?" Fargo asked.

Her eyes lifted to him. "I owe you," she said. "Damn near everything. You in a hurry to get someplace?"

"No hurry," he said.

Her mouth moved, a pleased, almost smug little smile touching her lips. She swung onto the horse, came alongside him, and the sun sent sparks from her flame hair. He took her to a place far away from the threat of Arapaho and the sweat of Conestoga-wagon people. "I don't suppose there's any chance of your staying around," she said as they rode. "We could make something good together, I think."

"You're beautiful enough to stay in one place for, I'll say that," he told her. "Maybe some day, when I've finished what I have to finish."

She nodded, quiet acceptance of a fact she'd already embraced. But in the sweet dark of the night, as he spiraled ecstasy for her, his firm strength full inside her, she clung to him and her words were breathed into his ear. "I never knew that paying up could be so good," she whispered.

"The collecting isn't bad, either," he told her, held her cream-alabaster breasts against him. Time and the trail could wait awhile.

LOOKING FORWARD!

The following is the opening section
from the next novel in the exciting new
Trailsman series from Signet:

THE TRAILSMAN #3: MOUNTAIN MAN KILL

*Summer, 1861, the north Wyoming Territory
at the foot of the Grand Tetons
and the Wind River Mountains.*

"Going to stay here a spell?" the girl asked, hope in her voice. The big black-haired man with the lake-blue eyes shook his head slowly and saw the moment of disappointment touch the girl's face.

"Sorry," he remarked, and she gave him a little half-shrug in return. She sat across the table from him in the town's only saloon and hotel, but she wasn't a saloon girl and he liked that. She was fresher, softer, more natural. And hungrier. That much had been in her eyes the very first moment they exchanged glances. That was only yesterday, he reminded himself, after he'd arrived in Wind River with the supply train he'd brought all the way up from Kansas. She was working in the general store when he had stopped there for saddle soap and there'd been no false coyness about her, and he liked that, too. She'd agreed to a drink with him last night without hesitation and now she was across from him again in the noisy saloon-lobby.

"Wind River isn't much of a town for staying in," he said quietly, and she allowed a small, rueful smile.

"I guess not. It needs a lot of growing yet," she said.

Skye Fargo glanced out the window behind where they were sitting. Her answer had been an understatement. The Wind River Mountains rose up just beyond the edge of the town, rugged, towering, glaring down. Two things came out of those vast mountains and onto the town. In winter, the roaring blizzards, and in the spring and fall, the roaring mountain men. Wind River was a fur-trading town, a place where the mountain men came to sell their precious pelts to the agents for the fur companies. The Rocky Mountain Fur Company had an agent in Wind River. Hudson Bay was thinking of one, he'd heard, but that company was plenty busy with the Northwest-Canadian territory. A handful of ranches bordered the town on the southern end, and a trail of silver miners used it as a stopping place. That was Wind River, a trading post masquerading as a town.

He brought his eyes back to the girl in front of him, Jenny Lindhof, a slender figure in red and white calico, small waisted, with breasts that seemed high and pointy under the folds of her dress. She had a face, small-featured, that bordered on being waiflike, yet was somehow very appealing, with hazel eyes that were level and forthright. Not really his kind of woman, ordinarily, yet something had sparked between them the moment they'd met. Besides, it had been a long, hard trip, too long without a woman.

"How'd you come to Wind River, Jenny?" he asked.

"I was in Dry Creek," she answered. "That's some sixty miles south, when my pa died," she answered. "He was a silver grubber. I'd no place to go and no money. When Mr. Axelson asked me to come here and work in his store, I just up and came."

His eyes studied her face for a moment. "You're a funny little creature, Jenny Lindhof," Skye Fargo said, not ungently. "You'd fit in at any church social, but you've come here with me easy as any dance-hall girl."

She gazed back at him as she thought about his words. "I guess it seems that way," she said. "My pa taught me to take things when they come your way. You're an uncommonly good-looking man, Skye Fargo. Most of those who come to Wind River are more animal than human. A girl gets tired waiting. Tired and feeling wasted."

Her small, thin-fingered hand disappeared under his as he patted it. "Your kind of honesty needs matching, Jenny," he said. "I'm not thinking about holding hands or long-time courtin'."

Her smile held something he'd never seen before: shyness and satisfaction at the same time. "I didn't figure you were," she said softly.

He leaned back, returned the smile. She was indeed a surprising little thing, this new friend, yet instantly likable, he decided, and that was rare enough, too. He turned, called the waitress over, and told her to leave the bottle. He glanced at four men coming into the big room through the front swinging doors and then returned his attention to Jenny Lindhof. He was pouring another drink for both of them when he became aware of the figures moving toward the table; he glanced up, saw the men bearing down on him. He put the bottle down and watched them approach. The first one was tall, swaggering, wearing hardness with the pride of the cruel. The three close behind him were sweat-stained cowhands, one with dull eyes, one with a flattened nose, and the last one slack-jawed, his eyes intent on Jenny Lindhof.

The hard-faced one halted as Skye sat back. "You Skye Fargo?" the man asked harshly.

"I might be," Fargo returned.

"I'm Brody, foreman for the Harry Stanton Agency. The boss wants to see you," the man said.

Fargo frowned, cast a glance at Jenny. "Who's Harry Stanton?" he asked, saw Jenny start to answer but the man's voice cut her off.

"Agent for the Rocky Mountain Fur Company," Brody snapped.

Fargo nodded, the name clicking in his mind. "Yes, I passed the place coming into town," he said.

"The boss said to bring you back with us," the man continued.

Fargo allowed him a tight smile. "Sorry. I've other plans for tonight. Try me in a day or so, if I'm still here," he said, and turned from the men.

He felt a hand come down upon his shoulder. "Tonight," the man said. "The boss sent us to find you and bring you back."

Fargo glanced at the man's hand, brought his eyes up to the man's hard face. He let Brody watch his eyes turn from soft lake-blue to blue quartz. "You've got a half-second to get your hand off there, cousin," Fargo said in almost a whisper.

The man hesitated, then let his hand drop away. "The boss don't take to being turned down," the foreman said.

"Then it'll be somethin' new for him," Fargo replied. He let his eyes flick over the other three men and then back to the foreman, saw the man watch his hand come to rest on the butt of the big Colt .45 in his holster. "Good evening, gents," Fargo said with cold affability. He saw the foreman, Brody, hesitate again, his hard face twitching, then watched the man turn, gesture to the other three to fall back. The quartet shuffled off and Fargo turned back to the girl. He heard the breath escape from between her lips.

"Exactly who is this Stanton?" he asked her.

"Mister Big in the fur-trading business. Most of the mountain men sell to his outfit," Jenny told him.

"How the hell did he know I was in town?" Fargo frowned.

"I guess you've got a name," she said.

The big, black-haired man gave a grunt. Her words were too true. He was always surprised at how many knew the name of Skye Fargo, the Trailsman. Too many, sometimes, such as just now. Too many who wanted his special talents, too many who'd heard too much, some of it pulled out of shape, some of it true.

"Let's go to my room, Jenny," Skye said, closing one big hand around the neck of the bottle. "We won't be bothered there."

The shy little smile came at once but she rose to follow him as he threaded his way through the tables of the hotel saloon-lobby. Foreman Brody and his crew had decided to drown their failure in a corner of the room, he saw, and he caught Brody's quick glance as he led Jenny up the stairs. His room was at the far end of a dim hallway, close to the top of the back stairway. He opened the door, turned the lamp on low and Jenny stepped inside. He saw her glance take in the only furniture in the room: a single chair, a battered dresser, and the brass bed. She turned, and he helped her take off the small shawl she wore about her shoulders.

Jenny Lindhof seemed suddenly so small, all the waiflike quality returning to her, and he found himself hesitant, her eyes giving him no sign. He saw no expectation, desire, no invitation, yet there was no reproof, either, just a wide and waiting expression. He was still trying to read her when she lifted herself up on tiptoe and kissed him gently on the mouth

"Thanks," she said, and he waited. "For not wanting to treat me like a dance-hall girl."

He smiled. "You're very different, Jenny," he said, leaned down, and pressed his mouth to hers. Her lips, thin, suddenly seemed to expand and her mouth opened, little pulling movements drawing him in deeper. He felt the fire flame at once in his loins. Slowly, he pushed her back onto the bed, set the bottle on the floor beside one of the brass legs. Her lips reached up for his again as he sat down beside her. Gently, he let his hand push the calico dress from one shoulder. Her hand came up and he watched her fingers pull open buttons. The dress came free, slipped from her shoulders altogether, and he pulled it down to her waist. The high, round breasts were no larger than he'd suspected, but still deliciously inviting, full and firm and fresh as new-bloomed partridge berries. Her arms came around his neck and he took one full little breast in his mouth as she pushed his shirt open and off. He unbuckled his gun belt, let it fall to the floor where he heard it slide under the bed.

He pulled gently on the breast and felt her back arch. "Oh, my, oh, oh, oh, my," she whispered in rhythm with his caressing lips. She pushed up to help his mouth take in more of her and he felt the rest of the calico dress slip off, paused, drew back for a moment. Her body was without an ounce of extra flesh, a young girl's body, flat stomach and long rib cage, but the dark triangle startlingly large and thick. She pulled his chest down atop her, his mouth back upon her breasts as she cried out again, small words of instant ecstasy. Her hands were moving down his back, nails tracing a sharp line that excited with its hint of pain. He didn't hear the click of the door opening as she ran little sounds together, but the harsh voice shattered the fevered beginnings with malicious delight.

"Now, ain't it a shame to break in on this," Fargo heard the voice say, recognized the foreman's rasp at once. He heard Jenny's gasp, felt her arms tighten around him, her body grow taut as a coiled spring.

"Easy. Relax," he whispered to her, and in a moment, felt her drop back onto the bed. He half-turned, his body still mostly over hers. Brody was standing with a revolver in hand, grinning, the other three behind him.

"That's right, Fargo, just back off the little lady," the foreman drawled.

"Yeah, let's have a good look at her." The flat-nosed one laughed.

Fargo didn't move, except to let his ice-blue eyes flick boldly over the three men.

"You ain't hardly started yet, anyway," Brody jeered. "You're out but not in." He laughed coarsely at his own words.

Fargo turned a fraction more, still covering most of the girl with his body. His eyes, blue slits, measured the distance to the gun held casually in Brody's hand. The other three had their guns still holstered.

"Get up, Fargo. You're goin' with us," Brody snapped, his voice growing hard.

"I'll stay here and finish for you," the slack-jawed one added eagerly. Fargo moved a fraction more. His right hand, half under his body, gathered the top bedsheet into a ball inside his fist.

"I guess you boys win," he remarked, and the men saw the powerful torso begin to slowly push up from Jenny Lindhof's nude body. Brody sneered as he grunted. He was still encased in his own smugness when Fargo's hard-muscled figure catapulted sideways and, with the same motion, snapped the bedsheet like a whip. The sheet wrapped itself around Brody's forearm and gun, and Fargo yanked hard at the same instant. The foreman jerked forward off balance and Fargo's left came around in an arc to catch him on the side of the jaw. The blow sent him crashing headfirst into the brass of the foot of the bed. He hadn't slid down to the floor yet as Fargo dived over him, crashing into the two nearest intruders. He brought both down with him in a tangle of bodies as the fourth one drew his gun in panic. Fargo rolled, seizing the slack-jawed one with him, as the shot slammed into the wood of the floorboards.

"Goddamn," he heard the man curse. Fargo, on his back, held the slack-jawed one over him with one hand around the man's neck. He twisted with his human shield as the gunman tried to find a clear shot; then, bringing up his other hand, Fargo pushed with all his strength. The slack-jawed man's body rose, arched backward, and fell into the other two, who twisted away in an automatic reaction. Another shot rang out, this one plowing harmlessly into the ceiling. But the Trailsman had bought the split second he wanted, enough time to reach the whiskey bottle and fling it. It smashed into the flat-nosed face of the one brandishing his gun out and the man staggered backward, shouting in pain, dropping his gun to wipe at the cascade of blood that erupted from his face.

Fargo dived again, low, slamming into the nearest pair of legs, and the man went down. Fargo swung at once, felt his hand connect with flesh and bone, heard the oath of pain. The man landed half atop him, and Fargo used his shoulders to drive him backward. He sank his fist deep into a belly made fat by too much beer and heard the man gasp out breath as he drew his legs up in pain, half-turning on his side. Fargo yanked the gun from his holster just as the foreman, Brody, pulled his bloodied head up. Fargo saw the man's hand come up with the gun in it, and the black-haired man fired instantly. The shot caught the foreman at the bottom of his neck and his head fell forward, driving the spurting red down onto his chest.

Fargo whirled, the bellow of pain and rage exploding to his right, looked up in time to see the flat-nosed man roaring at him, face streaked with blood, but the jagged neck of the bottle clutched in one hand. As the wild, red-stained figure leaped at him, the piece of bottle held outstretched in one hand, Fargo flattened himself to the floor, rolled, felt the man's figure catapult over him. He kicked out as the man's legs followed, flipped the figure upward. He heard the harshly guttural cry that ended in a gagging sound as the man came down on the jagged piece of glass in his own hand.

Fargo spun again, saw the slack-jawed one on all fours, shaking his head to clear it. The fourth man half-stumbled, half-fell as he tried to reach the door. Fargo leaped up, caught him as his hand closed around the doorknob. He slammed into the man with all his strength and heard the sharp crack of a wrist bone and the scream of pain that followed. The figure slumped to the floor, crying in agony, curling his legs up under him. Fargo turned from him, grabbed the last of the quartet, spun his slack-jawed face around. Stark fear was in the man's eyes.

"Jesus, no, don't kill me," the man sputtered.

Fargo kept his grip on the man. "I'd as soon put a hole through you as the other two," he rasped. "But I want you able to go back and tell your boss what his stupid gunslingers tried to do." He flung the man away, turned to the one holding his limp wrist in pain, rocking back and forth on his knees. He yanked the man forward, ignoring his cry of pain and fear mixed together, flung him half atop the slack-jawed one. "Both of you, take those other two with you. You'll find somebody to bury them. You tell your boss how it was, you hear me, bastard?" he barked, kicked the man in the leg. The man nodded vigorously as he pulled himself to his feet.

The sound of voices and footsteps gathered outside the door. Fargo found Jenny with a quick glance, huddled in one corner, her calico dress held in front of her, then opened the door. The hotel clerk, the bartender, and a half-dozen others had come upstairs.

"It's all over," Fargo said, stepped back as the two men dragged the body of the foreman out of the room, then did the same with the other red-stained, slashed body. "Some folks got the wrong ideas into their heads," Fargo said quietly. He saw the bartender and a few of the other men move to help carry the two dead bodies down the back stairs. The hotel clerk started to turn away when Fargo reached out to him.

"I'll need another room," Fargo said matter-of-factly. "This one's going to need a good cleaning in the morning."

The clerk stared at him for a moment. Wind River was a town used to violence, but this big black-haired man meted it out with icy efficiency. "Room Ten, just down the hall," the clerk said. "It's yours, sir."

"Thanks," Fargo said calmly, watched the man hurry away, and closed the door, turned to Jenny who still clutched the dress to her. "Slip it on. We're going down the hall to another room," he said. Her eyes, wide, unmoving, stayed on him, but he saw her shudder; he reached out to her, drew her against him, held her until she stopped trembling. He looked down at the round, hazel eyes. " 'Less you'd rather I took you back home," he offered, waited, retrieved his own gun and holster.

"I'd just sit there and still be scared," she said. She stepped back, slipped the dress on in one quick motion and followed him as he led the way down the hall to the other room. He closed the door behind him, bolted it this time.

"We won't be bothered again," he told her. She sank down onto the brass bed, almost a twin of the other one except for its own set of scratches. He sat down beside her and pressed her back onto the bed, kissed her gently. She made no response for a few moments, and then he felt her lips opening, growing softer, returning the pressure. He helped her wriggle out of the dress and undid his own clothes. His eyes took in the narrow-hipped figure again. Jenny Lindhof, naked, seemed more waif than woman except for the thick, luxuriant triangle. He bent down, gently taking one round, high, little-girl breast in his mouth.

Her gasp was instant, and he felt her hands press upon the back of his neck. He let his tongue move slowly in circles around the tiny tip, felt it harden instantly and once again she pushed upward to give him all of the breast. Her hands moved from his neck, down along his body, tracing a feverish path down to the risen shaft that waited her. As her hands closed around it, he heard her little cry of delight and she half-turned, drew her breast from his lips. She swung herself in a half-circle, head bent down to the male hardness of him, using both hands to caress and stroke. He heard the little sounds, almost a whimpered laugh, that came from her as she put her face against him, rubbed her cheeks over his eternal symbol. Then he felt the warm moistness enclose him as her lips caressed. Tiny sounds of delight came from her, pure and filled with pleasure and discovery. Finally she drew back, a shudder going through her body, and then he felt her legs moving over onto him. She lowered herself over him, slowly, crying out in ecstasy as she moved her torso up and down in her own rhythm. She leaned forward for him to pull upon the high little mounds and her hands played up and down his sides. He let her indulge in everything she wanted and he then rolled her to the side, then onto her back, and her legs clasped around him at once, drawing him into her with fervent anxiety.

"Oh, Fargo, oh, oh," she cried out with his every movement, words joining rhythm to form a song of ecstasy until suddenly she screamed and clasped herself to him, to cling there until the shattering moment subsided. She lay back on the bed, her eyes fastened on him, the shy little smile suddenly touching her lips, the hint of satisfaction in it once again.

"You're a surprising little thing, Jenny," he said, pressing his face against the high little-girl breasts.

"Make the most of your moments, Pa always said. You never know how long it'll be between," she answered. She lay beside him for but a short while and then she began to once more make the most of her moment, exploring pleasures in her own ways, a small, thin monument of high-wire sexuality. Finally she slept with arms tight around him until the morning sun rose high enough to slide into the room. He opened his eyes to see her devouring his body with her eyes. "Just want to make sure I remember everything," she said to him. Her fingers touched the half-moon scar on his forearm and her glance questioned.

"Bear claw, Grizzly," he told her and she gave a tiny shudder. She rose, up into a sitting position, brushing her breasts across his lips as she did.

"I open the store this morning," she said, swinging from the bed.

He watched her as she hurried across to the little bathroom, small, flat rear, all slenderness and almost boyish from the back. He heard her wash and then she came out, glistening, the lithe young-girl look of her terribly appealing. She slipped on clothes, stood dressed in moments, a smallish, very proper and demure-looking young girl, and he found himself thinking of Jenny Lindhof in the night. The outside of a package could certainly mislead one, he reflected wryly.

"When will you leave town?" she asked with her open, level eyes.

He shrugged. "Have to pick up the rest of my pay for the wagon trip this afternoon," he said.

"Then you're on your way?" she asked.

"Pretty much," he said, got to his feet, and went to her, cupping her face with one big hand. "If I stay, you'll be the first to know." She smiled. "You're an unusual little package, Jenny. Someone worth your while will pass through here someday."

"Maybe. Someday," she said. "Meanwhile, I'll have this to remember. I'll make it last. It was all it ought to be." She reached up, kissed him quickly, turned to the door. "Don't come to me 'less you plan to stay awhile," she said, pausing, her small face grave. "That'd be too much to handle."

"I understand," he said, and knew he'd abide by her request. She was too nice a person to use. She disappeared out the door and he dressed slowly, putting his gun belt on last. He emerged into the hallway, paused, his eyes searching the area. He didn't figure the two from last night to come back. They'd had more than enough. But they could have equally stupid friends. He moved down the hallway, hand on the butt of the Colt .45, relaxed as he went downstairs and paid the clerk for the room. The bar-lobby was empty save for an elderly black man sweeping the floor and one waitress cleaning tables. The sun, strong, now, came in through the windows. Fargo stepped outside, his eyes squinting down the main street of Wind River. A half-dozen platform drays lined up taking on supplies. Silver grubbers. They'd move on along the lower reaches of the Grand Tetons, searching, forever searching. Damn few of them finding.

Beyond the end of town, the Wind River Mountains rose up, an awesome green wall, vibrant and throbbing. The mountain men weren't the only ones who trapped and hunted the vast area. The Indians also hunted the Wind River Mountains, made summer camps in the fertile bountifulness, mostly Arapaho and Cheyenne, with some Poncas and Northern Shoshoni. He took his eyes from the mountains, started off the front step of the hotel to make his way down to the Two Fork Supply Company for the balance of his his pay for delivering the supply train from Kansas. He'd only taken a half-dozen long, loping steps when a woman's voice called out from behind him, a touch of arrogance in her tone.

"Mister Fargo! Just a minute, please!" the voice said.

The big man turned, pushed a lock of black hair from his forehead, and focused his gaze on the woman as she stepped from the edge of the hotel building. His eyes took in a tall woman clothed in a maroon silk jacket over a matching skirt. A full, deep bosom pushed out a white silk blouse from under her jacket. His eyes paused at her face, with even features, gray-blue eyes and a pair of thin high eyebrows that gave her an air of constant haughtiness. A good-looking woman, he decided, with her brown hair pulled back in a bun, good-looking and very self-assured, her gray-blue eyes doing their own piece of instant assessment. "I'd like to talk to you," she added.

"Seems I'm awful popular around here," Fargo remarked.

"I owe you an apology," the woman said. "I'm Caroline Stanton. I sent my foreman and his men to find you last night. I told Brody to ask you to come see me, that's all. The rest was his doing. He's always been a stupid man, forever needing to prove something. Frankly, I won't miss him."

"Me neither," Fargo agreed flatly.

Caroline Stanton offered a smile, coolly warm. "I apologize again for his actions," she said. "But I do want to talk to you. But not here. Will you come out to my ranch?"

Fargo eyed Caroline Stanton. In her early thirties, he guessed, the self-assured poise of a woman used to being obeyed. "I thought Harry Stanton was agent for the Rocky Mountain Fur Trading company," he said.

"My husband hasn't been a well man for over a year. I run the agency now. He only makes occasional trips down to Casper. He's on one now, in fact." Her eyes traveled up and down the big man's long hard frame. "Will you come?" she asked again. "I promise it won't be a waste of your time." The gray-blue eyes held his, eyes saying so much more than her lips. "Shall we say this evening?" she pressed.

He shrugged agreement. He seldom denied his natural curiosity, especially where good-looking women were concerned. For a grubby little trading-post town, Wind River was turning into an interesting place. Caroline Stanton read the shrug correctly and smiled. "Head west from town, take the road to the right out by the big oak," she said. "I'll expect you at eight."